Never Cry Alone

BY: Tyrell Plair

Plair
MULTIMEDIA AND PUBLISHING

NEVER CRY ALONE

A serial killer's deadly game pushes Tracy Lane to her limits as she fights to protect Atlanta's streets.

WHEN Amber Seasons, the daughter of two of the world's most popular reality stars, is murdered, the case lands on the lap of Tracy Lane and her partner Lewis Mitchell. Tracy is one of A.P.D's (Atlanta Police Department) most experienced detectives and has been solving crimes and witnessing travesties since the day she graduated from the police academy. Now, Lane and Mitchell are thrown into a real-life game of cat and mouse while working in the major crimes department. Atlanta is one of the deadliest cities in America and is filled with unexpected curveballs, twists, and turns. And that is just the tip of the iceberg in a truly dark world.

Soon after Amber is found, the body of another young woman is discovered, and the similarities are no coincidence. Faced with the reality that a serial killer may have taken residence, Tracy is forced to enlist the help of the G.B.I. (Georgia Bureau of Investigations), and the Federal Bureau of Investigations. With all of these resources made available to her, she still has no physical evidence to process, no clues, and no motive. She soon realizes that without a renewed strategy from the killer's eyes, the chances of stopping these killings will be impossible to stop.

Can Tracy Lane put an end to the homicides that are starting to make headline after headline in her city, or will Atlanta continue to have their murder rate go up by the week?

CHILLING. SUSPENSEFUL. UNFORGIVING

This book is dedicated to the hard work and effort put in by Tracy Lewis, my aunt, everyday as a law enforcement officer. Your work is appreciated, and I appreciate you.

Love your nephew,

Tyrell

CONTENTS

CHAPTER ONE

MISSY

Amber Seasons laid on the cold metal table in a new pair of underwear. Her body was as clean as she'd ever been in her life. Her eyelids were taped wide open, exposing the empty sockets that once held her piercing blue eyes. An Alizzyll-American volleyball player, with hopes of playing in the Olympics one day, laid dead on a steel gurney, while her extracted eyes stared back at her lifeless body on the table next to her.

I carefully dipped the tip of the paintbrush into the small vial filled with blood. With each stroke, I created a perfectly shaped teardrop on Amber's cold dead body. I leaned in close, blowing gently on my human canvas to speed up the drying process. I had to admit, this one was special, a reminder of the one that started it all. Amber was a carbon copy of the self-entitled brat who met her fate years ago, which is the reason why she was to be my masterpiece.

I was now done with my part in this sadistic ritual, it would be time for the finishing touches from my partner, Mister, soon. Reveling in the moment, I stood up and danced to the heavy metal song that played through the speakers. The demons that lived within my soul had become my friends long ago, and tonight, they danced with me.

"One with the night, I walk with the devil. My eyes are that of a

killer, so to death, say hello. Look at me now, your terror I feel. My hate runs so deep, and that's why I kill, yeeeaaaah!!" The lyrics to the heavy metal band blared throughout the room. I hummed along to the lyrics. I turned as Mister stepped into the room. He grimaced at the loud music, looked around, then inhaled deeply, taking in the scent of the room. As he drew closer, his mincing steps resonated off the walls.

I quickly noticed his attempt at a smile — an effort made awkward by the fact that half of his bottom lip was missing, distorting his expression. The huge cartoonish knot on his forehead, where a plate had been implanted, forced his left eye to squint. His distorted face turned the strongest stomach; however, his chiseled physique was the result of a daily training regimen that would turn every woman's head if they weren't privy to anything above his shoulders..

Injured in an explosion in Afghanistan that had nearly blown the right side of his face off, Mister became the object of finger pointing and peculiar stares. He grew tired of being the topic of conversations and the butt of jokes, which ultimately forced him into seclusion, until I found the monster. Most, who were now unfortunate enough to catch a glimpse of him, found themselves overwhelmed by discomfort, and he was usually the last face they would see before death.

I was the the sole person who accepted and treated him with basic human dignity, more than his own family who had shunned him, which is the very reason for his undying loyalty to his new muse. I treated him like a human. To the world, he was a grotesque creature: a war hero reduced to a sideshow oddity. But not to me… I was different. I became his solace, often easing his deep-seeded stress through murder or other malicious acts.

Our connection was born from darkness, a connection that only fate could provide. The women we abducted served as a twisted form of release for him. It was a form of a misguided quest for vengeance for the women that rejected him. Mister and I, bound by our understanding of each other's scars, found a disturbing remedy for our pain in the suffering of others. We were two souls, each marred by separate tragedies, yet we found perverse healing in the same cruel acts.

"She's ready for you now." I presented my masterpiece, looking at Mister for his approval.

"Are you alright?" Mister questioned, his words stumbling over each other.

"Just fine, why wouldn't I be? You, on the other hand, should be asking yourself that question," I added, handing him a pair of prongs.

Mister opened his hands, exposing two prosthetic eyes that he had sculpted for his new precious play thing. I smiled.

"Nice… She'll look stunning."

Mister mumbled something inaudible before walking over to the lifeless figure. He stared in amazement at my work, before continuing with his own ritual. After placing on a pair of gloves, he grabbed the dead girl by her jaw, then squeezed each one of the prosthetic eyes into its new home with the precision of a skilled surgeon. Stepping a few feet back, Mister inspected his handiwork.

"Hahaha," he laughed loudly. He always found how the women looked to be hilarious after he inserted their new eyes. The artificial eyes bulged out of the girl's eye sockets, which made her look excited or better yet, surprised. This provided Mister with childlike amusement.

"She's ready for you now." Mister pointed his arm out as if presenting a brand new car. He stared at the lifeless figure, and a cloud of sadness became evident in his expression.

"You liked her, didn't you?" I sought an answer, while changing my vocal tone as only a mother, or sister, would do with a child whom they cared for.

He nodded in reply, then lowered his head in compliance, knowing that I was in control at all times.

"I know. Finish, and I'll let you have a picture to remember her by, okay?" I proposed.

"She was not li-like the others," he countered.

"I know she wasn't, that's why I picked her. But like the others, she has served her purpose, and it's time for her to have her moment. You did a good job, but we need to go, so hurry now, we need to get going," I encouraged him.

Mister carefully positioned the dead girl's body, ensuring she was set at a precise right angle, as if she was ascending to the heavens. Mister then meticulously adjusted her eyes. I walked over to the counter and retrieved the ancient Polaroid camera with a melancholy smile and began snapping pictures, capturing the ethereal moment. The camera whirred before a film slid out from the camera's front, falling freely to the floor. I took several pictures until there was no more film left. I bent down and retrieved one of the photos off the floor, then handed it to him. Mister gently shook the portrait and watched as the image slowly came to life.

"Satisfied? Now, let's go," I ordered, before walking off.

Mister gently placed the photo down, a trace of regret flickering in his eyes, overshadowed by a determined acceptance of his orders. With a quick, efficient motion, he unlocked the wheels on the gurney and followed me out the door, not once looking down at his victim.

CHAPTER TWO
DETECTIVE LANE

Grappling with the familiar adversary of insomnia, I lay awake at three o'clock in the morning. My gaze fixed on the ceiling fan as it twirls in endless circles. Today was eventful to say the least, as I had to stop a couple from shooting each other in the gas station parking lot while I was grabbing a lottery scratch off ticket. I chose not to even file a report as neither weapon was loaded nor out of its holster.

In the soft hush of the night, one of my mom's favorite gospel songs whispered a gentle but persistent presence through the room. The soulful strains of 'Alabaster Box' by Yolanda Adams filled the air. I mouthed the words silently, a private communion in the stillness of the room. The moonlight was at full strength tonight, casting a nice illumination that was relaxing.

Night after night, my career as a homicide detective in Atlanta, Georgia, became the unwitting thief of my sleep. My therapist, with the best of intentions, often advised me to leave work at the office, as if my job was as detachable as a fast-food manager's apron. The true reality of my profession was far different. The cases and mysteries clang to me, inseparable from my thoughts, day or night.

I often wonder how any homicide detective could disconnect

entirely from the case after they left work, but still cracked the tough cases. I understood the wisdom in my therapist's words, the need for distance, but in the gritty reality of my world, such separation was a luxury I could seldom afford.

I chose to become a police officer, and on November 20, 2000, just three days shy of Thanksgiving, I mustered the courage to share this pivotal decision with my family. This was a conversation fraught with hesitation, delayed for good reason. The weight of their potential reactions had loomed heavily in my mind, a blend of concern and anticipation coloring my thoughts as I prepared to unveil a path that might reshape our collective future.

It was an uncomfortable truth that was often left unspoken, and in many families, including mine, there existed what could be loosely termed as the 'good' and 'bad' sides. This dichotomy, of course, hinged on one's perspective. The side of the family I grew up with, for instance, was more infamous than famous. Our conversations frequently revolved not around milestones and achievements but rather around questions like 'When is he scheduled to be released?' This query, loaded with implications, was a testament to the unconventional narrative that shaped our family legacy.

Despite their reputation as the less law-abiding members of the family, each one from this so-called 'bad side' possessed a heart of generosity. Contrary to what their actions might suggest, I can assure you that every single one of them wouldn't hesitate to give their very last possession to help someone in need.

When I finally broke the news to my family about my decision to become a police officer, their reaction was supportive yet tinged with caution. They embraced my choice wholeheartedly, but not without a warning: to be mindful of wearing my uniform in the presence of their friends. This advice, layered with unspoken implications, underscored the complex dynamics of my family's world.

More than 20 years have passed since that pivotal moment. Over these years, I have offered my family a new perspective on what it means to be a police officer. Through my actions and principles, I'd shown them the importance of conducting oneself with integrity and fairness, especially when entrusted with the responsibility of serving citizens from all walks of life. This journey was about redefining perceptions and demonstrating the true essence of dutiful service.

My sister, Leann, and I grew up immersed in a world shaped by my grandmother's words of wisdom. Instead of direct instructions, she spoke in quotes and slogans, weaving lessons into our daily lives. One of her favorite sayings, which has deeply resonated with me throughout my life, was "Help those in need and protect those who cannot protect themselves." These words became a guiding principle for me, a beacon guiding my path. It was this ethos, instilled in me since childhood, that ultimately inspired me to pursue a career as a Law Enforcement Officer (LEO). I reflected on those principles one night, amidst the quiet hours of the early morning, and I found a certain solace, even as I lay restless remembering the upbringing I was blessed to have because of my grandmother's love.

Laying in bed, my phone was my only companion in the dark room. I checked emails, social media sites, and text messages for what seemed like the hundredth time. Just as I sat my personal phone aside, finally feeling my eyes grow heavy, the sharp ring of my work phone shattered the silence. A brief glance at the caller ID revealed it was Mitchell, my partner of six years. As his name flashed on the screen, I began to brace myself for the impending bad news — a call at that ungodly hour was seldom a bearer of anything good. With a lingering thought of my grandmother's words, I answered the phone, ready to face whatever lay ahead.

"Damn it, Mitchell, always timing your calls perfectly to interrupt my rare moments of sleep," I answered with half-hearted humor. My voice, tinged with the fatigue of the late hour, carried a note of resignation - the life of a detective rarely allowed for uninterrupted rest.

For some reason, Mitchell found my response funny as I heard him snicker. "Well guess what? I was already in bed sleeping peacefully ten minutes ago when I got the call that I'm giving you. You can start getting dressed. I'm already heading to your house. GPS says twenty-five minutes."

Hanging up the phone without replying, I tried my best to prepare myself mentally for the day.

Four-twenty a.m. showed on the clock by the time we made it to the crime scene. The night was still very much upon us. A small crowd of onlookers congregated off to the far side of the road where the crime scene tape was sectioned off. Concern on the neighbors' faces wore heavy as they tried to figure out what had transpired in their quiet suburban community.

Mitchell and I exited the vehicle, accessing the crime scene immediately. As we approached the perimeter of the investigation, Mitchell reached out, gently lifting the fluttering ribbon that marked the boundary. With a practiced ease, I ducked smoothly under the lifted barrier. The simple yet familiar gesture, a silent dance we performed at countless scenes before, granted us passage into the heart of the crime scene. We walked past onlookers, excusing ourselves from answering any questions from the media.

"Hey, are you guys homicide? What's going on? Who got killed?" were some of the questions I heard in the faint distance as we continued to our destination. There was a street light that shined just enough for me to get a glimpse of what would seem like normal everyday faces to many, but to me, they were potential perpetrators.

The group that congregated that night appeared to be concerned citizens hoping that they weren't witnessing the demise of a neighbor or loved one.

"Good morning Detective, what a way to start the day, huh?" the uniformed officer stated without looking for an answer as he continued writing notes in his worn leather notebook.

"Morning," I stated flatly. *What was good about starting your day viewing a deceased body?* I wanted to say.

"Where is the first responding officer?" I questioned instead.

He raised his arm and pointed in the direction of a well-rounded officer, rubbing his head slowly and pacing back and forth. His stress level was evident.

"His name is Officer Millbrook, and I must say, he's pretty shaken up. Young fella must've not been around anything like this before."

The uniformed officer stated, giving us a good heads up of the young officer's mental state.

Mitchell and I headed in his direction.

"What do you make of what you've seen so far Mitchell?" I asked, getting his take of the scene.

"The first thing that I noticed was the four way stop, which means the killer or killers could have come and gone in either direction. I also know that the interstate is only a couple of miles away," he stated quickly before we made it to Officer Millbrook's location.

Standing about 5' 7", Officer Milbrook's stomach protruded slightly, and he rapidly rubbed his head, showing his obvious sign of nervousness. I could imagine him joining the police force as an obligation to his family history in law enforcement, more so than his willingness to protect and serve. His youthfulness was on full display as he looked in our direction and made eye contact with us. We walked over, and Mitchell did the honors.

"Officer Millbrook, I'm Detective Mitchell, and this is my partner Detective Lane," Mitchell stated as he extended his hand, trying to make the young officer feel at ease.

He was sweating profusely and given the low fifty degree temperature, I decided to check on the young man's well being.

"Officer Millbrook, are you okay?" I walked over and placed my hand on his shoulder.

He simply nodded, which I humbly accepted. "Good, now could you take us through what happened when you arrived on the scene? What did you do first?" I asked while Mitchell pulled out his notepad.

Officer Millbrook gave us a brief synopsis, then led us to where the victim laid. The sun was starting to peek its head, giving us an illuminated view of the suburban neighborhood. This quiet community, nestled in its seemingly perfect and meticulously manicured reality, was unaware of the turmoil brewing beneath its serene surface. Little did the residents know, their illusion of tranquility was on the brink of shattering. As the sun climbed higher, reaching its zenith, the full scope of the tragedy became glaringly evident.

"A four way stop...upper middle class...corner easily visible by only one house," I spoke into my recorder as we walked to the victim. Mitchell donned a pair of gloves before bending down to uncover the body.

"Jesus, Lane, what in God's name?" he shouted, letting the sheet fall back onto the victim's face, then promptly stood up.

Mitchell waved his hands back and forth in front of his face, wafting away the putrid smell currently attacking his sinuses. I observed him cough several times as if he ingested the stench. Finally, he caught his breath. Mitchell donned his mask and composed himself.

The smell of bleach finally began to tingle my nostrils. I bent down and peeled back the sheet and looked down at the pale white skin of the victim; the realization that sunlight was in abundance hit me. The smell from the body forced me to don my mask as well. Once on, I then advised the other officers in the vicinity to do the same. The smell was so strong, she could have been soaked in bleach for what could have been hours or days. She was laid there, spread out in a pose as if she was an oversized porcelain doll. She had perfectly sculpted red lips, and she was positioned with eyes focused on us. She had some exquisite facial features, which I now noticed.

"Lane, look at her eyes," Mitchell suggested. I stopped my visual examination and froze when I realized what I was looking at. At first glance, one would think that you were looking at the biggest pair of green eyes you would ever see. But upon further study, you'd realize they aren't real. They were artificial, with markings underneath.

"These are manmade eyes, Mitchell. It looks like they may belong to some sort of doll or something. Do you see these markings on the face? I'm not sure what to make of them. If I were to guess, I would say that they are meant to be tears. But I don't get paid to guess," I let my observation be known with a small quip at the end.

Mitchell stood up and pulled his gloves off, along with his mask, giving a facial expression I've seen too many times in the past. He was concerned enough to give me pause in my gut.

"Something is not right about this Lane, her body has been soaked in bleach for who knows how long. It seems like someone is trying to get rid of the evidence. Then, the sadistic removal of her eyes... What is that all about? This was not a kill and dump. No, there is something more sinister going on here, I can feel it."

I heard Mitchell speak before a series of loud pops and screaming ensued.

There was nothing for us to hide behind, other than our victim. So we dove to opposite sides on our stomachs, using the eloquently laid out, dead porcelain doll to provide as our sole protection. Both of us quickly pulled out our weapons and scanned the entire area for the direction of fire. I looked over and noticed blood seeping from Mitchell's left pant leg. Focusing on where the small crowd once stood, three teenage kids on bikes laughed uncontrollably. It was evident by their demeanor that they were the cause of the disturbance.

"You, crazy sons of bitches! You assholes could've gotten someone killed. Get the fuck out of here before I have you locked up for obstruction. This is a fucking crime scene!" the young officer that we had just spoken to moments ago snapped using hand gestures.

I stood up, holstered my weapon, dusted off, and composed myself instead of responding frustrated as the young officer did. Slowly, I began to approach these young men to see what they thought was so funny about the situation.

"I must say, given the circumstances, fellas, that was not cool," I stated, beginning to make out the faces of three teenagers looking to be no more than high school seniors or recent graduates.

"I know this is strange and interesting, something I hope you guys have only seen on television, but your actions are adding to the chaos. Tell me, what are you three doing out here on bikes popping fireworks so early in the morning anyway? Before you answer, know that what the officer said is true about being charged with obstruction."

I watched as each switched their resting legs holding their bikes. Each kid was apprehensive. I recognized their body language and how they wanted to flee. It was as if Mitchell read my thoughts because I watched his large hands grab the handlebar of one of the teens.

"You wouldn't be thinking of trying to run off before she finishes what she has to say would you? Because that would be disrespectful... Right?" Mitchell questioned.

In unison, they all replied, "Yes, sir!"

"Continue, Lane, I'm sure that you have their undivided attention now."

"Thank you. Now, as I was saying. Did any of you see, hear, or notice anything this morning that didn't look right? Maybe it was a vehicle you hadn't seen around the neighborhood. Someone who looked creepy or odd from this past week that might've seemed kind of questionable?" I continued.

They all shrugged their shoulders and one by one stated that they are back on spring break from college and just out pranking. When they saw the crowd, they decided it would be an easy target. None of them realized it was a crime scene. I asked them a few more questions concerning the culture of the neighborhood. I wasn't too familiar with the area and needed to get the lay of the land, so to speak. Some of the reports from the neighbors that officer Millbrook spoke to had stated that it was a quiet, upper middle-class area. I ensured Mitchell had no further questions and then dismissed the teens. They would be of no use to us. Almost immediately, I heard someone call out my name.

"Detective Lane, we have a witness," the unfamiliar voice called out. I walked over to the officer.

"Who is it, and where are they?"

"I have to tell you, she is not all the way there if you ask me," he added as he twirled his fingers around his ear to describe her mental state. "She lives right up there." He pointed out.

"Thank you, we'll take it from here," I told him as I began to navigate up the steep steps that led to the front porch.

Upon reaching the porch, I noticed two oversized rocking chairs that looked like they hadn't been used in years. One had a pair of boots sitting right under them, with a cane leaned against it. The other one had a plaid throw blanket laid neatly upon the armrest. The French-Creole style home design, at one time, had to be the pride of this neighborhood. I watched as a senior woman came from behind the semi-dusty screen door with a huge smile, which I hoped she wouldn't say she witnessed the crime. It was a smile that displayed her lack of having guests; she was excited.

The woman held a small, excited dog in her left arm that barked incessantly trying to greet us. The senior woman extended her frail hand, which bore a few dark blemishes associated with old age. Her handshake was firm, and she formed a smile that most people that don't have their dentures in usually show, which was still warm and welcoming. I studied her briefly. I could tell that she didn't sleep much, the puffiness under her eyes told the story. The wide-eyed gaze that she wore probably only lasted until her next cup of coffee or the prescription that she might need to help get through the day.

"Good Morning, my name is Detective Lane, and this is my partner, Detective Mitchell. We'd like to ask you a few questions."

"Of course, come on in, why don't you? My name is Gloria Anthony, and this is my little one, Chloe," she stated, referring to the small Havanese puppy, as we followed her into her home.

CHAPTER THREE
DETECTIVE LANE

The house was immaculate, a stark contrast to the exterior, which looked as if it hadn't been kept up at all. We entered the living room where I could've sent the best forensic team to comb, but not one speck of dust would've been located. Sitting by the window was a chair. Mrs. Anthony was sure to take up residence there most of the day when she wasn't cleaning.

"Could I offer you detectives some tea or water? I don't have much else, but some moonshine… Oh my, did I say that out loud?" she questioned, giggling as if we were still in the prohibition era.

The officer's words lingered in my head about her mental state not being all the way there, but at that point, I hadn't been able to make that assumption.

"We are all good, Mrs. Anthony. We would like to ask you a few questions if you don't mind," Mitchell replied in a harsher tone than intended, I'm sure. I could tell that she may have taken his statement the wrong way, which told me to intervene before we deterred our only witness.

"On the contrary, Mrs. Anthony, I would like a glass of tea, and I'd like a little honey instead of sugar if possible, thank you," I said.

Her facial expression softened, and she flashed a brief smile. I watched as she rinsed the large mug out and placed it next to a raw honey bottle. "It shouldn't take long, sir, are you sure you don't want anything?" She made another heartfelt offer to Mitchell, which showed her maternal and caring instincts.

"No, thank you. I'm sure, Mrs. Anthony. Do you mind if I ask you a few questions while you prepare the tea for my partner, ma'am?" Mitchell questioned as he pulled out his notepad, his vocal tone much softer.

"Sure, I can walk and chew bubble gum at the same time too," she retorted jokingly, which produced a much-needed laugh. I still couldn't understand the officer's statement about her mental state.

"Mrs. Anthony, could you tell us what you heard this morning, or saw that might be helpful with this investigation?" Mitchell began his query.

"Of course, sir, just a second," she replied politely. I studied the elderly woman as she moved gracefully around the kitchen in no hurry to answer Mitchell's question until she was done. Mrs. Anthony handed me the teacup with a matching plate, set a bottle of raw honey in front of me, and then proceeded to prepare her own cup of tea.

I tracked her walking back to the oven, and something caught my eye. I nodded in the direction of the empty chair that sat opposite the refrigerator within arm's reach of the oven. The comfortable-looking chair was not one meant for dining, but more so for comfort.

It had a men's blazer draped across it, which I would bet the farm was her husband's. Visualizing him coming home from work and making this his first stop was easy. I imagined he would walk in, and give his wife a warm hug and kiss before taking a seat in that chair as she prepared dinner. In turn, she would hand him a nice soothing cup of tea to enjoy, and they would both inquire about the other's day and make small talk until dinner was done. My creative fantasy about their life was cut short when Mrs. Anthony sat down next to me.

"I saw you looking at that chair, Detective Lane. If you were wondering, that chair is where my husband would sit while I prepared dinner."

I caught the past-tense reference that she made. Her response let me know that this wasn't her first time explaining that to someone. Mitchell and I both gave our condolences; I couldn't imagine losing someone that I truly loved.

"Now, I won't go so far as to say that I saw anything, but I did hear something," her statement took Mitchell and I both aback.

"Now, Mrs. Anthony, when you say you heard something, are you saying someone told you about what happened this morning?" I inquired, hoping that it wasn't the case.

"Oh no, ma'am. I didn't hear anything in that sense. I heard a loud vehicle around 3 a.m., that's what I meant to say. It had an unusually loud sound that we, I mean, that I haven't heard around here before… Well, at least not in these parts. I knew today was not trash day, and even so, they would never pick up that early. You see, I walked over to that window right there." She pointed to the window. "And that's when I saw something laid out on the ground. I figured that someone had either fallen off the vehicle or jumped out. Either way, it didn't sit right with me, so I called the police." I could tell that she was very observant.

"Mrs. Anthony, were you able to get a good look at the vehicle, its make or model maybe?" Mitchell probed on. He had now moved to the edge of his seat, becoming more engaged in our questioning.

"I didn't get a look at the make of the vehicle, but I do know that it was an old model dually truck. My brother had one back in 1995, and it sounded just like the one he owned. Heck, I almost thought it was him, but he's been dead for ten years now," she proclaimed.

We offer our condolences once again as it was starting to seem like everyone that she told us about was deceased. Mitchell noted what she had told him, and then he immediately stood up. I followed suit; there was little left to learn from Mrs. Anthony, at least for now.

Exiting the home of Mrs. Anthony, I noticed the entire scene grew immensely while we interviewed Mrs. Anthony, to the point that three officers were now stationed near the crime scene tape. The crime scene was being processed as instructed, which I expected. I saw the Fulton County Chief Medical Examiner, Aneesa Leggett, in a conversation with one of her technicians. She noticed me as well and both of our faces lit up with joy.

Aneesa and I met when I was in the ninth grade at Booker T. Washington High School. She was one of those girls who played every sport and was into every school club that most young girls strayed away from, such as chess club, debate team, and Beta Club to name a few.

Aneesa would literally leave basketball practice some days, head to a chess competition, spend an hour at the local library reading about human anatomy, and then she would cap her day off with an evening jog alongside her autistic brother, whom she takes care of 'til this day.

"Hey, girl. Oh my goodness, I was not expecting to see you here this morning," I said, hugging her briefly. I thought that you had that appointment with Darren today?" I questioned after we broke out of our embrace.

"I did, but Darren was adamant last night about not wanting to go see his therapist. He has a software project that he is so focused on. Can you believe that he has a secret room in the basement that he's put together so no one can see his work? I'm like WTH? At this point though, Tracy, whatever occupies his time in a good way, I'll just accept it. Hi, Mitchell!" she acknowledged him, finishing her sentence, then they exchanged handshakes.

"What did you make of our victim, Doctor?" he questioned, knowing that if anyone had seen or heard of anything like this, Dr. Anessa would be the person. I am taken aback as her facial expression changed to a look of concern, a rare look for her.

"To be honest, I don't want to speculate anything at this time. I can't tell you the time of death, due to her body being preserved and the tampering of evidence from the bleaching of the body. I will have to do a thorough autopsy which will require some time. There are no obvious signs of death, no ligature marks on the neck, and no noticeable blunt force trauma. I am positive about one thing though, the removal of her eyes was done postmortem, most likely right after she was deceased for them to almost look real. I just gave my team instructions to get our victim back, start a toxicology report, and I will perform the autopsy myself hopefully tomorrow," she relayed.

I was thankful that she would be performing the autopsy. "I have a question. Have you experienced examining a body being doused in bleach, or should I say soaked, like this victim may have been?"

"I have witnessed people using a number of things to conceal evidence, and yes, bleach was one of those methods. Just give me time to do my thing, please. If there is any evidence there, I'll find it as you well know."

With that being said, there was nothing left for us to do but to try to get some rest. This was about to be a long day, I was sure of it.

CHAPTER FOUR

CARLA

The loud music resonated throughout the speakers electrifying the entire class, as the instructor brought our class to an end. This by far was one of the best classes that I've been in. Zumba has helped me with my focus and coordination. I have gained strength, and my highschool baby fat is now gone.

"One, Two, Three, and Four!!! Game time ladies, great job every-one!" Our young vibrant instructor screamed over the music. "What a great way to end the week, is it not?" The class roared with applause, giving the instructor her answer.

I sat down on the floor next to my best friend Jessica, while hugs and well wishes from the other ladies went around. "Damn class got a little extreme tonight, huh Jess?" I wanted to see if she enjoyed it as much as I did.

"Extreme" is an understatement. We went four minutes past our stop time… that's like another mile of sprinting." She replied. She did have a point.

"If you only knew, Jess. I'm really on a mission this year. We're ranked in the top ten in the entire country, and as a freshman, the bonus has been placed on me to lead us to a championship, or at minimum a conference championship… Can you believe that?" I told her, having already embraced the challenge ahead of me.

Jessica looked at me, and I could basically read her thoughts. We had been friends since before we could talk. "Carla, you are a once in a lifetime player. What some would call a 'Generational Player' with the potential to shatter every freshman batting record that exists."

"Thanks Jess, but you don't know how much pressure I have on me at times. I know that I handle it well, but all of the people know me, and to be honest, I love it!"

"You're fucking right you do!" We high-fived each other.

"Who wouldn't want to be a preseason first team all-american, and with this NIL (name, image, and likeness) deal that I was able to garner, life couldn't be better. Sometimes, I can't believe this journey is real."

"Hell, I can believe it. On a serious note, whether you win a championship this year, win player of the year, or whatever you're going to be nominated for, stay true to yourself. I, for one, know nothing will change with us, but I don't want you to… you know…"

I knew what she meant, she was talking about being like my parents. "Thank you, Jess. I know that you will never tell me what I want to hear, but always what I need to hear. You never have to worry about me changing, or switching up on anyone, it's not in my character, although it may be in my blood." I set the record straight that my parents were just that, parents. Our paths coming up were very different. Things that they had to do to become the individuals they wanted and needed to be had nothing to do with me.

"You're right, I hope you didn't take what I said the wrong way." She had a solemn look on her face.

I pulled my keys out of my purse. "No, it's fine. I don't like to be compared to my parents, and that is one of the reasons I have been able to excel in my own lane, because it is different from what they did growing up. Anyway, enough about them, the parking lot is getting thin, let's get out of here. Are you still coming by for dinner tomorrow?"

"Have a nice night ladies," our instructor shouted our way as she headed to her car.

We both spoke back, letting her know how we were looking forward to our next class. "I'll have to pass on the family festivities, but I'll give you a call in the morning just in case you feel like running," Jess countered, knowing that a morning run was not my thing.

"You're hilarious, Jess, I'm not getting up that early on spring break, or any other day to run miles; I like to run in the evenings. I do have to get going, Scott is probably wondering where I'm at as we speak."

"Yeah, he is a worry box, but for good reason though. It's a dangerous world out here," I told her as we embraced. "You let me know when you've made it home Jess, and I'll do the same."

I headed in one direction and watched as Jess made it to her car which was near the front. I waved at her as she passed me by. I held my car keys in my hand tightly as I tried to remember which aisle I had parked on. The parking lot was sparse with only a few cars left, so I hit the alarm on my key fob and saw the light on my car notify me where to walk. There were a couple ladies sitting inside of their car. We waved at each other before they pulled away. I kept walking, with only maybe a few feet to go to get to my car, when I noticed a woman standing with the hood of a truck open. She wasn't part of our class, so she must have broken down here. I kept walking toward my car, then paused as I looked around the parking lot. It was now, only her and I as two cars pulled away in unison.

"I should've known not to take this stupid fucking truck!" I heard her say aloud. I looked to see if someone was with her. I peered into the truck cab as much as I could, and it was empty. I pulled out my phone, then headed across the parking aisle to where she stood. She acted as if I had startled her when I approached her.

"Excuse me, do you need any help?" I offered. The woman jumped out of her skin.

"Oh my goodness, you scared the shit out of me!" She held her hand over her heart.

"I apologize, I didn't mean to scare you. It looked as if you needed some help, and with the parking lot empty, I wanted to offer a hand."

The lady paused then studied me briefly, she was maybe in her late thirties or early forties, I guessed. "Unless you're a certified mechanic, then you probably can't help me, but thanks though," the woman replied.

"Well, I'm definitely not a mechanic, but you don't look like you're one either."

"I'm not. My name is Missy, and this here is the piece of shit truck that I bought for my ex-boyfriend that I unfortunately had to repossess. It's ironic that the truck broke down just like his cheating ass after I put my foot to his balls." She was vicious, I had to admit. "The fucking asshole."

"I'm Carla. Have you already called for help or a ride? If not, I don't mind giving you a ride to the nearest gas station. It's not safe to be out here alone," I told her, concerned for my safety as well.

"You might find this hard to believe, but do you know that I had to get my truck back because I caught naked photos of him and another woman in the phone that I paid for? And get this… he busted up the phone after he snatched it out of my hand." She was obviously upset, and crazy to be buying a man a truck and a cellphone.

She also acted as I had all the time in the world. I had the mind to Facetime Scott, and inform him as to what I was doing. "Hey, I'm supposed to meet someone shortly. I know you're upset, so either you can use my phone and call for help, or I can take you to the nearest gas station."

"Why is it that men can't accept breaking up without being a total dick?" I knew now that she had been drinking, and I couldn't blame her after her night. "Hey, what did you say your name was? Carla, right? Carla, I just might have no choice but to take you up on your offer. Let me at least try to crank this piece of shit up before I just leave it here. I would hate for you to have to drive me to the gas station, if you don't have to."

At this point, I just wished I had kept walking and ignored the woman. I was growing very impatient. I was starting to feel like aborting this good Samaritan mission altogether. My grandmother's words came into my head just as I had thought about walking away. "Always put yourself in others' shoes, Carla." She was right. How would I feel if I were stranded in a parking lot and someone didn't offer to help. "Ok, let's get it over with, what do you need me to do?"

"Thank you, this shouldn't take long. All I need you to do is climb into the truck and turn the key when I tell you to. If it turns over and starts, cool. If not, I'll give you gas money to drop me off." She made it sound simple enough, so I placed my phone in my back pocket and my car keys in my front pocket before climbing in the driver's seat.

Missy gave me a convincing smile, before holding her hand up like they did at races, and yelled out the words. "Try it now!"

I immediately felt a large hand grip the back of my head, and a damp rag was forced against my nose and mouth. I struggled to remove the large hands, but he was too strong. I could feel his breath on my neck, and I wondered why I hadn't seen anyone in the cab of the truck. My last thought, before I began to lose consciousness, was how I should have followed my first mind, and not my grandmother's.

CHAPTER FIVE

MISSY

I walked into the room, and I felt the terror radiating off the young woman that we abducted. Mister stood over her with his arms folded, his imposing presence looming in the shadows.

"Let me talk to her alone, my love," I instructed him. Mister bent down as if on command, and I planted a kiss on his forehead, and he then left the room, as if in a love struck trance.

"Why am I here?"

"Such impatience. So what's the problem?"

"Problem? You have the nerve to ask me what the problem is, you fucking bitch. You and that monster of yours is the fucking problem!" the woman retorted with venom in her voice, which I found justifiable. At the same time, I had to let her know who exactly was in charge.

I moved with the speed of a wrestler, and before she knew it, I had her in a choke hold. The young woman gagged once, then her eyes bulged as she was unable to breathe.

"I'm sure you don't understand your situation, young lady. This is not a game, and I will not tolerate your disrespect. Is that understood?"

She tapped my arm in submission. I continued to apply pressure making her unable to wither a word. "Is that a yes?" She tapped my arm faster. I released my grip, then pushed her away from me. "Next time, I'll snap that neck of yours."

I watched as the young woman tried to catch her breath, before speaking.

"Why-why are you doing this to me? If it's about obtaining money, my family has plenty of it, so you-you don't have to do this, I promise you. I won't tell anyone, just please let me go." Her pleas were worthless in my eyes.

"Predictable…so fucking predictable. You definitely have assured me that you are the spoiled little bitch, I knew you to be when I first saw you. You people think that money gives you a sense of entitlement. You think that waving your money, status, or credit card makes everything go your way. Well, guess what? You didn't think I knew who you were, did you?" The look on her face was priceless.

"You could have all the money in the world and it wouldn't get you out of this situation. It's time that people like you receive the judgment that you so often dish out. You need to understand that even when you have what *you* deem the perfect life, it can all change in the blink of an eye, like now. I'm that change, *Carla*." I could feel the lust to end her life prickling my skin.

"Please, whatever happened to you, it's not my fault. My life is not perfect, I can assure you. I help people all the time… Please don't think that I'm like how you described me, or someone made me out to be." Tears began to roll down Carla's cheeks, which only made my power over her rise.

"Don't worry, you'll be able to help many more through your martyrdom. I don't know how long you'll be here, but this is your home until that changes." I walked over to where Carla sat looking as sombering as anyone could look.

"I'll do anything you want, just please let me go. Please! It's cold in here, I haven't used the bathroom, and I'm thirsty. I just want to go home."

I reached out and stroked the girl's face. She was a beautiful creature, full of life, and she had grit. I moved my hand down her neck, leading to her trembling breast.

"Relax Carla, I'm not going to touch your breasts. You don't like being touched by another woman, I take it."

Carla closed her eyes, not hiding her disgust. I leaned in close to her face allowing her to feel my breath on her earlobe. "I don't care what you like, that is what you will soon learn." I continued to guide my hand down past the young woman's navel into her soiled underwear. The sobbing began and a smile formed on my face. I penetrated Carla's softness with a forceful push, and a slight gasp escaped her mouth.

"Stop it! Get your hands…" She struggled to squeeze her legs in her own way of self defense, as tight as she could, hoping she could snap my wrist.

I pulled my hand out of her and licked my fingers. I saw the disgust on her face.

"Not bad… Not bad at all. I'll be back lil' lady… Don't go anywhere," I joked before backing out of the room and securing the steel door. The lights shut off after my exit leaving Carla to contemplate my next move, I was sure of it.

CHAPTER SIX

DETECTIVE LANE

Sitting on my couch after finally taking a brief nap, I feel refreshed. Mitchell had dropped me off earlier, once we concluded our initial investigation. We were waiting for the preliminary reports, which would give us a moment to catch up on a little sleep. I stood up to stretch when the house phone rang. I didn't have to guess who it was at this time; I already knew. I smiled hard before I answered. "Hello," I managed to get out before I yawned and stretched.

"Good morning, Mom. Why are you sounding like you just woke up?"

"Because I just woke up. How are you doing, June? I thought you had a test today?"

"I did, but that was like three hours ago, Mom."

I looked for my cellphone to check the time. Once I found it, I flipped it open to discover it was noon. My feeling of refreshment made sense now. I couldn't remember the last time I slept five hours straight. I was sure that I had missed several calls already.

"What class is this test for?"

"Psychology. It's the last prerequisite that I have."

"That's great." I took a deep breath before continuing. "June, I was just assigned a case that may occupy a lot of my time." I had to throw it out there as she had planned a visit soon.

"Mom, your cases never impede on what we have going on. Why would this one be any different?"

I pondered her question for a second before I responded. "I really don't know why I said that other than a gut feeling this case might be time consuming, and just to let you know. We both look forward to your visits, so that's why," I said.

I could hear June take a deep breath, followed by a brief silence, a bad trait handed down by me that I had also inherited.

"I can stay with my friends if it's an issue. I'll see you when you have time then, Mom," she stated matter-of-factly.

"Look, June, I know you're upset...well, disappointed. But just know, disappointing you has never and never will be my intention. You know just as well as I do that sometimes cases get closed quickly, but more times than others, they don't. All I'm saying is that I may have to immerse myself in this case. I hope that it won't affect your coming home as scheduled. I'm sure that we will be able to find an activity or two to enjoy while you are home unless you'll be too busy," I told her, finally able to take a breath as I stood up and stretched.

"So, you're going to use my words against me in this case, huh? How typical, Mom," she replied before laughing. It was a much needed laugh to break the tension for both of us.

"I am very well aware of your job and what it entails. I'm a twenty-one year old raised by the ever-evolving Tracy Lane, so I can handle myself. I have plenty of friends in Atlanta so being bored is the least of my worries. All that matters is that I get to spend a few quality hours in the presence of my favorite person in the world, binge watching forensic files or In Living Color."

I wished that she could see my smile. June never ceased to amaze me. She had a way with words that I could most definitely say she got from her dad, but with a caring nature. That was a gift from me, passed down from my grandmother. "You are your mother's child, June. I can't wait to see you," I said with all sincerity.

"Okay, Mom, I have to get going. Take care of yourself and enjoy your day…and tell Mitchell, I said hi. I love you."

"Okay, I will, and I love you more."

I hung up the phone and immediately stared at it, anticipating the missed calls and texts from my long nap. **Meet me at the capital ME's office ASAP!** was the message that stood out. It was from Mitchell, breakfast would have to wait.

I literally took a bird's bath, got dressed, hopped in my car, sped down I-75, and headed to the Medical Examiner's Office as if I was late for a job interview. Mitchell was one of the most impatient people in the world and had already sent five text messages. There wasn't any sense in responding, I surmised. I'd see him soon enough.

My mind was floating on a spiritual cloud, so I decided to listen to a little gospel. I activated my app through bluetooth, and the sounds of Tasha Cobbs' *"You Know My Name"* resonated throughout the speakers. I found myself at peace, singing along with her word for word. I was not an avid Christian, but I did believe that a higher power watches over us. Sometimes, for the good of things, that higher power intervened. In this profession, I found it hard for anyone to believe that a loving God would allow some of the things I'd seen to happen to innocent people, young and old.

Mitchell was walking out of the front door when I pulled into the 'Reserved for Law Enforcement' parking spot. He was coming out of the medical examiner's entrance walking briskly. In frustration, he pulled out his phone and slung one hand frivolously in the air. My phone rang instantly. I wanted to laugh so bad, but I held it in, and answered his call.

"I'm here, watching you throw a temper tantrum, Mitchell. Is Dr. Leggett in?" I questioned without giving him a chance to speak.

"Lane, you truly frustrate me sometimes. Now, can you get out of the car so we can see what's going on? By the way, did June make it in town yet?" he questioned further, confirming June's theory that I never paid her any attention.

"Mitchell, how do you remember that June is due to come home this weekend?" I watched him laugh as I exited my vehicle.

"You forgot, didn't you? Huh?" He continued to laugh.

"I did, and she feels some type of way too," I relayed to him as I made my way across the street in his direction.

"Oh, wow. Sorry to hear that, Lane," he stated wholeheartedly.

We entered the heavily sanitized building that bore the faint scent of death, a fragrance that you would never forget once introduced to it. Walking past the receptionist's desk, Mitchell secured us both coffee, and we continued to the *"Room of Death,"* as some officers labeled it. It was the room where they performed post-mortem examinations. A (D.I.S), Death Investigation Specialist, stood by the scrub sink washing her hands. A portion of her blond hair peeked from under her bouffant surgical cap. She turned slowly upon noticing us enter the room. Drying her hands slowly under the blower, she smiled before walking over to us.

"I'm Detective Lane, and this is my partner Detective Mitchell," I introduced us both.

"Good Morning. I'm Kasey. Dr. Leggett has a court appearance this morning and requested that I walk you through things. She has already sent off for a toxicology report and advised me that she will be performing the autopsy tomorrow." The young protégé of my friend spoke so eloquently, her soft voice was welcoming. She maintained her smile as she relayed the message that the good doctor left.

"Sounds good. So, what else do you have for us?" Mitchell questioned, his disappointment in not meeting with Dr. Leggett evident.

"What else?" she repeated. Her tone mimicked his tone as she shrugged her shoulders. "Well, I guess, if you follow me, I can introduce you to Ms. Amber Seasons. She is well known here in Georgia," she relayed.

We followed her over to the gurney. Kasey peeled back the sheet slowly, exposing our young victim. The deceased woman looked exactly as we'd found her yesterday, other than a few marks on her body that were highlighted by Dr. Leggett or her assistant.

"Did you just say that her name is Amber Seasons?" I questioned.

"Yes."

"Please don't tell me that this is the famous reality show surgeon's daughter. Are you sure she was just brought in yesterday?" I asked, knowing that the chances of our victim being in CODIS (Combined DNA Index System) would be slim to none.

"In the words of Simon Phoenix, 'Exactimundo!' Amber Seasons is indeed the daughter of two of Atlanta's most prominent orthopedic surgeons. They are known for performing orthopedic surgeries on their reality show as a husband and wife duo. They perform procedures on professional athletes and stars from all over the world! They are so cool!" she exclaimed excitedly. "I would love to meet them…under different circumstances, of course. Cool fact, the Seasons actually performed Tommy John Surgery on my cousin, who is a pitcher for the New York Mets."

"That's great to hear, and your use of the quote from the movie "Demolition Man" is the only cool thing about that story. With all that being said, you still haven't told us how it came to be known who our victim is," I reiterated to her.

"Oh yes…that part. I was getting to that. I actually just found out not long after coming into work. Since I arrived at the office late, I decided to go through this week's missing person report while I awaited your arrival, and it's a good thing I did. Her parents reported her missing three days ago."

Kasey continued to spout technical terms and gave us the facts and evidence. Based on Kasey's findings, our victim was indeed Amber Seasons. This now took on a whole new level of exposure. I began to think about all the reality stars who put all of their business out there and didn't care what the world saw or knew. I would hope that the Seasons weren't the type of people to exploit their daughter's untimely death for ratings. My mind quickly started to visualize this murder investigation playing out in the media due to our victim's parents being well known.

"So, has the family been notified?" I queried, already knowing the answer.

"No. Dr. Leggett did mention that you would probably want to deliver the news yourself, Detective Lane. I can't imagine delivering that kind of news to a parent. It's hard enough just watching some of them view the bodies that come through here," Kasey expressed.

"It is a very tough thing to do, and it never gets easier," I declared, dreading the impending news that I was about to deliver. Kasey's head dropped momentarily. When she spoke again, the liveliness was gone from her tone.

"I have some photos that Dr. Leggett asked me to provide you. They are photos to present for identification purposes to the Seasons. I haven't looked at them. As I stated before, Dr. Leggett will be performing the autopsy tomorrow," she relayed before holding a medium size manila envelope that Mitchell quickly confiscated.

"Is everything alright, Kasey?" I inquired, noticing the sudden change in her demeanor.

"I'll be okay. It's just that I have watched their reality show for the last five years. I've watched Amber grow from a middle schooler to a star athlete in college. I just can't imagine how devastating this is going to be for them."

I took a deep breath before grabbing her hand in a show of acknowledgment. "Kasey, this is a cruel world, and tragedy doesn't care who it befalls. Just continue to do the things that will keep yourself from being in this young lady's shoes. Thank you for being so transparent and helpful today. Please tell Anessa, I mean Dr. Leggett, that I will look forward to her call." I released the young woman's hand then exited, with Mitchell walking beside me.

CHAPTER SEVEN

MISTER

"Mister, how about you go make sure the room is ready, I'll wait here," Missy told me, her voice steady and composed. I loved taking directions from Missy, it was the way she communicated with me. It was a stark contrast to what I was used to.

"I will be right there." I struggled with my speech at times due to an injury obtained in Afghanistan.

I was raised in a chaotic environment, and after high school, I couldn't wait to join the military. I had so much rage built up inside me, that I needed a place that would allow me to release it in a legal way. I gave eight years of my life to the Marines as a sniper. I enjoyed Afghanistan and being able to take out targets that were an enemy to our great country. But, I soon found out that once the military can't use you, they discard you.

I was sent on a mission to where I would have to be dropped off by helicopter. Our chopper was hit with a close range missile that sent us crashing to the ground. The pilot and copilot died on impact. The soldier next to me was still alive, but barely, as his seatbelt had cut into his neck. A fire began to form in the cockpit, and I knew that it wouldn't be long before it blew, or worse, the enemy caught up to us. I was able to remove my knife, cut myself loose, then free the soldier next to me.

My face was wet to the point I could barely see. I wiped my face, then pushed open what was left of the door. As soon as I got out and began pulling the soldier out, my sleeve caught on fire, and from there, it was as if the fire was consuming my entire face. I ran in a direction away from the impending explosion, then fell on the ground, and began rolling around in 120°F sand.

I managed to get my shirt off before the fire could make it to my lower body, then slung it as far as I could. My face burned something awful. Without thought, I used the water in my canteen that was strapped to my belt and flushed my face with it. It felt as if the skin melted away from my face. I grabbed a handful of sand, which at that moment felt cooler, and patted my face until the burning subsided. I lost consciousness shortly after, and was thankful that when I woke up, I saw a sleeve with the United States flag on it.

I had obtained severe burns to my face and upper body, from sitting next to the reserve fuel tank during flight. With broken ribs, burned hands that led to deadened nerves, I was now useless as a sniper. I was released back into society and told to blend in however I could. So as I had said when I left for the marines, I had no family to go home to. I would never return to that abusive household. I'd rather die.

I looked up at the monitor above that showed footage of every room and hallway in our secret facility. Missy was pacing back and forth growing impatient, she confirmed it when she looked into the camera and tapped her watch. I grabbed my gloves, then headed to her location.

"The Room," as it was aptly named, had state of the art equipment that you would find in a community care center. It was a meticulously prepared workspace where our twisted plans came to life. We had military grade equipment that allowed us to do surveillance and stay undetected where we resided. "The Room" was the final stop for each victim to be prepared for their final public viewing.

Attention was something most of these victims amassed, and Missy was a master at ensuring that each victim looked their absolute best. In her mind, she was doing them an honor by leaving them in a beautiful state to be remembered, while also sending a message.

"Glad you could make it. As you can see, our friend is resting peacefully in the corner. We have things to do; it will be dark soon. I need you to go through the checklist and start the preparations. I'll be back in a few minutes."

"Okay," I simply responded, then began what brings me joy. I started gathering the tools necessary for our impending ritual. Just as a nurse would do at a hospital, I sterilized the room and then dressed in some clean scrubs.

Missy reentered the room a few minutes later, and I could see by the look on her face that she was happy with my preparations. "The Room" had brought out the savage beast that she was always willing to release.

"Is everything ready?" she asked.

"Yes, the tools are ready."

"Good to hear. I'll be back shortly…and please behave yourself."

I nodded and watched Missy as she walked out of the room again. I loved the way her hips moved with each step; it left me in a trance at times. We had a lot of things in common, like her being a workout enthusiast; it helped us have a great relationship. I only wished that she knew how much I loved her, although I knew she could never love or be attracted to anyone like me. I was an eyesore to most, and my mental health made me very unpredictable, except with her. No woman wanted a man they had to take care of constantly, but that's exactly what Missy did for me. That was why I would forever be indebted to her. I owed her my life, literally.

I broke my thoughts and focused on the task at hand. I was left alone with the terrified girl, who laid naked on the cold gurney. She had finally awakened from the sedative I gave her.

"Hey, are you cold?" She shook her head no, then turned head away from me. I knew that to be a lie as she was shaking, but tried to be strong. I grabbed a sheet out of the linen locker, then laid it across her. I saw that she was thankful for not having to be exposed and stopped her from freezing.

"Thank you," she said, then turned her head away from me once again.

I pulled my hoodie off of my head and walked over to her. I kneeled down next to the young woman, my movements slow and deliberate. She forced her head as far as she could away from me.

"Are you afraid of me?" I didn't necessarily need an answer. I caressed a handful of her hair, leaning in close to inhale the scent that still lingered from her previous life. It would soon be gone.

"Leave me alone… I have been good like you told me to be."

"And you have, and that's why you are still alive. Do you know what's about to happen to you?" I dragged the words out with my lips close to her earlobe. She began squirming as if she could go somewhere. "Hey, hey, relax." I stroked her cheek softly with the back of my hand.

I could only imagine the thoughts that went through her head with her eyes squeezed shut. Whether she knew it or not, I would be the last man that ever touched her in this way. I began to grow an erection as her trembling was enticing. I was just about to explore her body more when I heard Missy abruptly enter.

"Hey, what are you doing?" She walked over to where we were. I placed my hood on.

"Nothing, she was cold," I managed to say, which was not a lie. I knew not to lie to Missy.

"You better not be in here messing up our rituals by being undisciplined." She reached up, grabbing me by my hoodie, pulling my face down close to hers and looked into my eyes for any hint of deceit. Missy never let me touch any of the women until she said so.

"I didn't." She let my chin go.

I was relieved when Missy turned her attention to the young woman. "Hey Carla, I just wanted you to know that your time here is coming to an end. We have an array of things at our disposal to ensure that you will look your best upon leaving. Mister, let's leave her here to get some rest. Give her another sedative," Missy instructed me.

I did what I was told under Missy's close observation. I knew that she didn't trust me around the woman that we kept. After completing the task and making sure that the woman was out cold, I followed Missy back to the office.

"What did you do to her?" Missy questioned me with a sinister smile on her face.

"Nothing, until you say so." I gave the only answer she expected to hear.

"You like them all, don't you?" she stated more than questioned as she approached me. Missy stood, then reached up her hand, rubbing it gently across my face.

I had a love-hate relationship with how easily she made me melt in her hands. "I-I don't like them all," I replied as I closed my eyes and inhaled the fragrance that lingered on her wrist. I had always envisioned having rough sex with Missy. I wanted her to feel every inch of me, and I wanted to also inflict the same kind of punishment that she allowed me to do to the women we captured. Her soft caress turned into a forceful grip on my chin with both of her hands.

"Good...because the last thing you need to be doing is getting attached to one of these things," she informed me. "Furthermore, you know they care nothing about you. They secretly despise and have a deep reverence for someone like you. They don't know the person that I know, and they never will. In this world, it's all about looks...superficial vices that lure people in." With a soft push away from me, she removed her hand from my face after making her point. She turned and pressed her butt against my midsection.

Missy was good at playing games, so I wasn't surprised that after scolding me that she would try to entice me. She loved to get me worked up for the other women, but I wanted to know when I was going to be allowed to explore her body.

"Stop playing," I whispered as I placed one hand around her neck and used the other to grab her waist. "You always tell me you care, but not like I do."

Missy looked at me, not saying a word. I lowered my hand to her butt and rubbed gently, then squeezed. She did nothing. Missy relaxed into my arms, which caught me off guard. I had never touched her in this way, and it made me uncomfortable, so I let go of her neck and backed away from her.

"I know what you're saying. You mean a lot to me too. I didn't grow up in a place where affection and love was shown," she confessed. "And, don't ever think I'm going to play games with you, that is not how I operate. I have somewhere to be, and I'll be back shortly. The girl has had enough for the day, so leave her alone. I promise you that you'll have your chance. Am I clear?"

"Yes," I told her, realizing that I just wanted her to leave. With that being said, Missy walked out of the office, leaving me to honor her wishes.

I kept my eyes glued to Missy's frame until she was no longer in sight. I had never defied anything that Missy had told me, but I was enamored with Carla Mango. As soon I saw on the camera that Missy was gone, I was going to pay the young woman a visit.

I gripped my manhood aggressively, adjusting myself, before heading back into "The Room." My erection was pressed up against my pants, and it leapt for joy at the sight of Carla. I was as happy as a kid in a candy store when I saw that Carla was lying in the same place I'd left her, resting as peacefully as possible.

"I'mmmmmm back!!!!" I did my best Jack Nicholson impression from "The Shining," while trying to nudge her awake. The woman's eyes began to flutter while she tried to wake out of the sleep induced trance that she was in. "There you go…wake up. I need you fully invested because we are about to have some fun," I told her before removing my pants.

CHAPTER EIGHT
DETECTIVE LANE

The ride to Sandy Springs, Georgia became a tour of massive homes overlooking the Chattahoochee River. The overly priced homes offered everything that the imagination could provide, from massive statues with flowing water to private gates that gave hints to say "no pictures" and "I like my privacy."

Any other day, I would have enjoyed the scenery, but my mind wandered. Mitchell parked directly in front of the Seasons' home and began gathering his things from out of the back seat while my daydreaming subsided.

"We should've parked in the driveway, Mitchell." I started exiting the vehicle and realized just how massive these homes really were. I looked around and couldn't help but wonder how it felt to not have to worry about money.

"I wouldn't want anyone parking in my driveway to deliver me some bad news," Mitchell retorted.

"Really, Mitchell!? Like, what difference does it make? Bad news is bad news. You do see how far that walk to the front door is, don't you? I would hate for your plantar fascia to flare up. I don't want to hear the foot pain complaints on the way back to the precinct," I told him, being honest.

"You're right, Lane. Get in, I'll drive us up," he quickly responded. I lean into the passenger window and smile. He looked at me, confused. "I know that face. What is it, Lane?"

"Nothing," I replied.

"What is it, Lane?"

"On second thought, I think we should take the scenic route. You never know, our investigation could begin and end at this location," I pointed out, trying to be optimistic.

Mitchell reluctantly exited the vehicle. "This is a really nice piece of property, huh, Lane?"

"I was just thinking the same thing. It's a bit much for me, but nice nonetheless."

From our approach, we could see the massive forge-blended Cherokee stone pillars that became a staple of home improvement upgrades of the rich and famous. Even with the obvious heavy traffic that I was sure came with reality television, the Seasons managed to keep their property perfectly manicured. We continued our trek slowly up the driveway. I watched as Mitchell walked over to where a piece of orange tape laid flapping slowly in the wind, as if beckoning for someone to inquire about its reason for being there.

Upon further investigation, I noticed that there was construction tape lined along the driveway with the initials TLP in bold letters. Two Porta Potties sat spaced approximately ten feet apart, with one being distinctly different, which gave me pause to believe that one of those was specifically brought in for females or supervisors.

"Dang, Lane, do you think the Seasons use a golf cart to check their mail?" Mitchell questioned, as we began our trek up the long driveway.

I hesitated briefly before I answered, taking in how much farther we had to go until we reached the front door. "I would imagine so. Who would want to walk down this long driveway on the regular?"

"I'm sure they delegate those chores out to the kids," Mitchell countered, without considering the fact that we were going to tell the Seasons that they had just lost their only child.

I gave Mitchell a side-eye look, and he quickly picked up on why I had that look on my face.

"Hey, you can't expect me to remember that they only had one kid when this is like only our second day ever hearing about them." Just as he finished his statement, I tracked a red and black golf cart with several small to big-sized Georgia Bulldogs logos plastered all over it descending upon us.

"Looks like we have company approaching, Mitchell."

"I told you that they have a golf cart," he boasted.

"And you were right. I have your cookie in the car," I joked.

The golf cart pulled within 5 feet of our location and then stopped. A tall, slender, built gentleman wearing a pair of overalls exited the vehicle. His clothing was stained, and he had a rag in his hand that looked like he had wiped over a thousand oil dipsticks on it. Obviously, he had to be a mechanic or handyman.

"Can I help you folks?" He paused and looked us over before continuing on. "You do know this is private property, right?" he stated more so than questioned. I could literally hear the wheels turning in Mitchell's head.

Mitchell lived for people trying to flex the private property thing, when in reality, a murder investigation trumped any privacy one might think they deserve.

"As a matter of fact, you can help us. We are here to meet with the Seasons. You can start by alerting them to our presence, if you don't mind," he suggested pulling out his badge to display. "I'm Detective Mitchell, and this is my partner Detective Lane."

The worker's facial expression changed from one of protecting someone else's property, to one of panic. "Is everything alright? Is this about that little girl of theirs?" he questioned with genuine concern.

"I'm afraid we can't provide you with any information, but if you could alert the Seasons to our presence, it would be greatly appreciated," I told him.

"Oh yes, ma'am, that's not a problem. If you want, y'all can hop right on back, and I'll drive you right on up to where they are. By the way, my name is Jed. I have been working for the Seasons for over ten years. Things haven't been the same around here the last few days," Jed stated somberly.

Mitchell and I jumped onto the back of the golf cart and held onto the handles. With no regard for his passengers, Jed took off through the property.

"Could you elaborate on what you mean by things not being the same around here the past few days?" I asked, while Jed made his way around the side of the massive home.

"Well, I only know that a missing person's report was filed. They came out a few days ago and ordered all work on the property to cease and for everyone to go home. I just hope that nothing has happened to that little girl. She is their pride and joy. Well, we're here," he stated, bringing the cart to a sudden halt. "You can take those few steps right there and see them sitting at one of the tables."

"Thank you for your help, Jed. Listen, I'm sure hoping that you will be around just in case we need a ride back to our car," Mitchell suggested, half joking.

"That shouldn't be a problem. It is a long hike down that hill. Just ask one of them to notify me. They know how to do that very well," he replied.

His statements lingered in my head briefly as I made my way up the short row of steps with Mitchell close behind. "Mitchell, why do you think he refers to them as 'them' in that tone and, not to mention, the 'they do that very well' part?"

"Well, they're 'reality stars,' right?" He used his hands to make quotation marks for emphasis, while making his face look rigid.

I was just about to respond when a stunning middle-aged woman appeared out of nowhere. She was standing at the top of the stairs in a matriarchal way.

"Greetings. I'm Mrs. Seasons. I was made aware that you are looking for my husband and I," she spoke so eloquently with a radiating voice that reached us as we ascended the steps.

"Good morning, Mrs. Seasons. This is my partner, Detective Mitchell, and I'm Detective Lane," I managed to get out as the short walk up the steps took little effort. Her facial expression remained stoic. "If you don't mind, we'd like to speak with you and your husband briefly," I said without emotion.

"Is this about my Amber?" she questioned, barely above a whisper. At the mention of her daughter, she didn't offer a handshake as she spoke; I probably wouldn't have either. Neither Mitchell nor I replied. "You may follow me," she said.

Mrs. Seasons led us through a series of outside dining tables. She moved in a controlled manner, as if cameras were following her, which I'm sure by now was pretty normal for her.

Her husband was sitting alone when we approached. He peered over the newspaper he was reading. Upon noticing us, he began folding it neatly. He placed it on the table and continued to observe us in silence. He peeled his designer shades off his face in a slow motion as he stood up and adjusted his clothing.

I took in the casual appearance of Mr. Seasons and realized that he probably was barely seen like this. He was wearing a long-sleeved polo shirt tucked inside a pair of khaki pants, accentuated with a pair of VANS shoes. Something told me that this was his way of dressing down.

"Good morning," he greeted, before extending his hand. "Or should I say good afternoon?" He looked at his watch, which was probably muscle memory, then smiled. Mr. Seasons wore a smile that I was sure wasn't his original one, and possibly could have cost upward of a four-year school tuition.

"Good morning," Mitchell responded, extending his hand back to shake. "I'm Detective Mitchell, and this is my partner Detective Lane. Do you mind if we sit down and talk?"

"Sure. We can sit over here." Mr. Seasons gestured to a table a few feet away from the one he just got up from.

"Would you guys like something to drink? We have any Coca-Cola product you can think of," Mrs. Seasons offers with a hand on her husband's shoulder. "Howard secured a marketing deal last year with them," she boasted in a way that didn't seem offensive due to her graceful nature. By the way she carried herself, I would find it hard to believe that she'd ever been in any sort of conflict.

"A bottle of water for both of us will be just fine," I answered.

I intended to wait for both parents to be present before we started this difficult conversation. However, Mitchell seemed to have other ideas.

"What are you doing?" I whispered, but he didn't hear me.

Mitchell then placed a manila envelope on the table, its contents marked by the medical examiner's seal and bore the name 'Amber Seasons' on the front. I almost lost it. Mr. Seasons caught my eye and gave a simple nod, his gaze filled with sorrow. He then stood up and turned his back to us. With a theatrical stretch and a yawn, he appeared to be bracing himself for the impending news. His shoulders began to sag under the weight of his grief, and then he exhaled a loud, weary sigh.

As I watched the heart breaking of Mr. Seasons right in front of me, a loud crash caught all of our attention, even startling Mr. Seasons. The sharp, jarring noise of breaking glass made us turn to see Mrs. Seasons standing behind us with her hands covering her face. She was shaking with the kind of uncontrollable grief that only a mother could feel. Her eyes, filled with pain and disbelief, became fixed on the envelope that Mitchell had made available. Mrs. Seasons quickly focused on the name of her only child printed boldly on it.

I noticed that blood slowly dripped from Mrs. Seasons's hand as she stood silently with her hands still near her face while she stared at her husband.

"Mrs. Seasons, you've cut yourself," I said aloud, and moved in close to see the extent of her injury. "Mitchell, hurry up and search for something to slow down the bleeding!" I ordered.

Mr. Seasons turned around, wiping tears away. The strong and confident man we had just met moments ago was now gone. I couldn't imagine how he felt, but at that moment, he was of no use to me. I grabbed an open bottle of water off the table where Mr. Seasons previously sat, then walked over to Mrs. Seasons.

"I need you to take a seat. You're bleeding." She looked at me questionably, but did as I instructed without protest. Mr. Seasons, seemingly out of his trance, walked over and sat down next to his wife, then held her tightly in his arms.

CHAPTER NINE

DETECTIVE LANE

"Helen…Helen, are you ok?" Mr. Seasons questioned, while he slowly stroked her hair. I became aware of the glass fragments around his wife's feet. I looked around for Mitchell. *What is taking Mitchell so long?* I asked myself while playing the role of EMT.

"Mr. Seasons, there's glass beneath you guys. Could you please elevate your wife's foot so I can ensure there isn't any glass stuck inside of her shoe or foot?" Mr. Seasons nodded, then removed his arms from around his wife. He placed her legs gently across his, then elevated his feet in the chair next to them.

"Thank you." Mrs. Seasons looked down at me with her eyes full of tears, the sadness and hurt evident and radiating off of her. I met her gaze with compassion and empathy. Only a mother could understand carrying a child for nine months, bearing that child, and then the pain of losing one.

Before the moment became awkward, Mitchell had finally returned. He was out of breath, but I was thankful for his presence. "What took you so long?" I inquired. Mitchell shook his head, then bent down next to me.

"I ran into Jed while I was searching for a towel out by the pool, and he gave me this," he stated, handing me some non-latex gloves, a towel, and a first aid kit. "Do I need to dispatch EMS, Lane?" he questioned, not knowing the extent of Mrs. Seasons's injuries.

I looked up at the grieving couple. "I don't think so… just take care of her hands while I check her feet."

After placing on the latex gloves, I began to slowly pour the water on her feet as I felt for glass, while Mitchell attended to the wounds on her hands. "Mrs. Seasons, there isn't any glass in your foot, but if you'd like us to dispatch EMS, please let me know," I offered, leaving the decision solely up to her.

"If there is not any glass in my foot, I'll be fine… I apologize for earlier. It's just…" Her voice trailed off. "It's just that my Amber had so much going for herself, and now I don't know what I'm going to do." I stood up, removed my latex gloves, and tossed them on the table; I was sure they would be disposed of later.

"Mrs. and Mrs. Seasons, as you may know, my partner and I came here to discuss the disappearance of your daughter, Amber. I apologize if this meeting has started off the wrong way." I held out my hand for Mitchell to pass me the envelope. I then placed it on the table directly in front of me. "It is with great remorse that we have to show you these photos. I want you to know this may not be your daughter, but…" I caught myself and slid the envelope over to them.

The Seasons looked at the envelope as if it were laced with poison, then at each other. Mr. Seasons caressed his wife's face gently with one hand, then pulled a piece of hair out of her face with the other. A smile formed on his face, one that I have seen many men put on in this situation, trying to be strong for their loved ones. So often, their love for the person that is still alive made them try to absorb all of that person's hurt or somehow alleviate it. She returned her husband's smile and closed her eyes while he kissed her forehead.

Surprisingly, Mrs. Seasons retrieved the envelope, then slowly pulled out one of the photos and placed it on the table. The initial photo was only a headshot for identification purposes, to my relief. The couple glanced at each other, then at us. Our answer, and their worst nightmare, had just been confirmed; there was no need to see any more photos. Mrs. Seasons grabbed her husband's shirt tightly and buried her head. Her sobs were muffled, but loud nonetheless.

"I know this is probably not a good time, but in lieu of everything that has transpired, it is imperative that we ask you a few questions before leaving. Especially now that you have confirmed the identity," Mitchell announced to no one in particular.

"No... Now is not a good time!" Mr. Seasons barked, surprising everyone with his tone. "Now, if you don't mind, you can show yourselves out," he ordered.

"Now, you wait a damn minute, Howard!" Mrs. Seasons interjected, spinning around to face us with tears still running down her cheeks. "I don't know about you, but I want whoever did this to our daughter caught. If that means talking to these detectives all night, then I'll do it!" she emphatically stated.

Mr. Seasons threw up his hands in defeat, stood up, then began rubbing his head in frustration. "As my wife stated, we would like to help in any way that we can," he reluctantly offered. "I apologize."

"Thank you, but there's nothing to apologize about, we understand. Now, this first question may sound cliche, but is there anyone that you can think of that would want to hurt your daughter?" I began.

"No, of course not... Why would someone intentionally..." Mr. Seasons's voice trailed off as he thought about the statement he was about to make. Someone, in fact, had intentionally hurt his daughter. And, as in most cases, there was the possibility that the victim knew her killer.

"Amber was such a sweet girl, everyone loved her," Mrs. Seasons followed up.

"I don't question whether your daughter was well liked by everyone, ma'am, because usually when that is the case, you have more people that don't like you than you know; they just don't come out and let it be known. So, can you tell us if she had a boyfriend, or someone that she hung out with on the regular?"

The Seasons looked at each other briefly, contemplating their answer.

"She has a...friend, his name is Dexter," Mrs. Season replied subtly, removing the boyfriend title from association with her daughter. "Dexter wouldn't hurt a fly, not to mention, he doesn't know that my Amber is even missing," she inferred, still referring to her daughter in the present tense. "He left the country with his parents on a trip to Paris over a week ago for spring break, although his plan was to go to Florida with Amber, but his parents convinced him otherwise. Maybe he could've protected her had he been here," she deduced.

"Or even worse, Mrs. Seasons, he could've ended up a victim himself." I had to add clarity to her statement, especially since she said that Dexter wouldn't hurt a fly. "How often did Amber visit from college?"

The Seasons looked at each other again, pondering the right answer, which I'm sure came from being on their reality show. Every comment had to be approved through subtle looks and gestures.

"Doctors," I referred to them by their titles to let them know this was not part of their reality show. "The only way we can get started with investigating properly is if you provide us with what you can, and nothing more," Mitchell pleaded.

"Right. Our daughter usually comes home every other month because she plays sports. Over the past three months, she's come home at least once, if not twice, a month," Mrs. Seasons stated.

"Did she reside here when she visited home, or with Dexter?" I probed more.

"She stayed at home, of course, why?" quipped Mrs. Seasons.

I stood up before responding. "We need to see her room, if that's possible."

Mr. Seasons glanced at his wife with a request for approval on his face. He laid his eyes on her hand, which was now bandaged as good as any licensed practical nurse could have done.

"I'll be alright, Howard. You can go ahead and take them up. I will be right behind you. I'm fine." Mrs. Seasons looked at her husband with insistence in her eyes. He did as his wife requested. It felt a little awkward at the level of control that she effortlessly yielded.

We followed the grief-stricken father through the large house until we came upon a door that I assumed was their daughter's room. Mr.

Seasons stopped within inches of the door, then stuck his hand out, placing it flat against the door, as if feeling for a heartbeat. His back was still facing us, but that didn't distort the sobbing that could be heard. It was disheartening. My emotions began to get the best of me.

Mitchell placed a hand on my shoulder, and I realized that my mind had been heavily on my daughter. She was around Amber's age and also a college student. That was a coincidence that didn't sit well with me. Mr. Seasons finally found the courage and proceeded to turn the glass door knob that made a slight creaking sound when disengaged from the frame.

The cold breeze from the air conditioner rushed out of the room, enhancing the chilling feeling I already had. Mr. Seasons looked back, signaling with his head, beckoning us to enter first. I pulled out a pair of nonlatex gloves; Mitchell followed, doing the same as we went into the room cautiously. I could hear Mrs. Seasons creeping up slowly behind us.

The sunlight shone brightly through the blinds as we entered the room, causing me to shield my eyes. Mr. Seasons walked over, then quickly closed them, encompassing the room with a dim light. "Thank you, Mr. Seasons."

Suddenly, there was a scream that startled everyone in the room. We turned around to see Mrs. Seasons covering her face, looking down. I followed her gaze. Somehow, a photo of their deceased daughter had made its way out of the envelope that Mitchell held upside down, loosely in his hands. Mitchell tried to retrieve the photo quickly, but it was too late. Mr. Seasons picked up the photo and held it face down so that his wife wouldn't be able to see it.

"Howard! Oh my God, what is that? Is that?... Give it to me!" she yelled as she stood breathing hard. Her husband grabbed her, clutching tightly, doing his best to comfort her.

He held the photo tightly to his side, that was until Mitchell eased it out of his hand. A wave of emotion took over them as tears fell uncontrollably. I could no longer contain my emotions either. I used the back of my hand to stop the tears slowly falling down my eyes. Mr. Seasons led his wife over to the bed, sitting her down with the care of a nurse.

"Hand me the photo, Howard," she urged him again.

"Helen, don't…" he pleaded in a whisper.

"Howard, it's okay. I need to," she spoke convincingly.

Mitchell reluctantly handed the entire envelope containing the photos of their daughter to Mr. Seasons, which he, in turn, handed to his wife. They began removing the photos one by one, starting with a family photo that included the now grieving couple and their deceased daughter at one of Amber's softball games. She looked to be around 13 years of age in the photo, I surmised through the brief look I could see before the picture was buried in Mrs. Season's chest.

"Is this really necessary right now? You did your job by delivering the news, now if you don't mind, my wife and I could use some privacy," Mr. Seasons expressed.

Mrs. Seasons raised her head, wiped away her tears, then stood up. The room went silent as we stood, awaiting her next move. She walked over to the closet door and then opened it. "Amber only likes to do sports-related activities when she comes home. She either went to her old high school to train or to the gym." The strong woman that I had assumed her to be was now back.

Mitchell pulled out his notepad. "On the night of your daughter's disappearance, did she go to train at the high school or the gym?" At that moment, I realized the difference between the two.

I continued my visual examination imagining the young woman sitting at her computer desk, staring out the window at a lovely view of the backyard. The room was painted all white with deep red borders, which were colors used to accentuate the University of Georgia logo that was perfectly painted on the ceiling. Above the queen-sized bed on the shelf, adorned more of Amber's alma mater paraphernalia, along with a wooden sign that read "Education Over Athletics."

"I'm not sure about her whereabouts that night," Mrs. Seasons continued on as she made her way over to where I was standing. "Amber made that when she was in the sixth grade." She pointed to a wooden crest of sorts. "She is such a little tomboy. Howard was the only person that could really bring the little girl out of her," she shared her memories with the smile of a proud Mom.

I couldn't help but notice that she had repeatedly referred to her daughter in the present tense from the time we arrived. I'm sure it would take her a while before that would change. "Your daughter was a very accomplished athlete, and obviously talented in other areas such as art," I told them, genuinely impressed.

"Yes, she is… Oh, wow! Now I know exactly why I opened that closet," Mrs. Seasons interjected as she made her way back over to the open closet. She walked inside, and we all heard a scream, one that we had started to become accustomed to. We all rushed inside the large walk-in closet, almost simultaneously.

"Hey, is everything alright?" Mitchell questioned with his weapon drawn, scanning as if it were a secret entrance of some sort inside.

"Relax, Mitchell," I suggested. "Did you find something, Mrs. Seasons?"

Mrs. Season stood with her back to us, but we could see exactly what she was staring at. Mr. Seasons walked over to her side, fully aware why his wife had reacted the way she did. He picked up a large gym bag, then held it tightly to his chest, mimicking his wife's gesture earlier. He proceeded to exit the closet, and we followed closely behind his wife. He took a seat on the bed, then set the bag down in front of him before slowly unzipping it.

"Why is this here, Howard… Why?" Mrs. Seasons yelled at the top of her lungs, showing that side of herself that people rarely saw on the reality show.

He slammed his fist down on the mattress, causing several of the stuffed animals that were on the bed to fall to the floor. Tears began to surge down his cheeks. Mr. Seasons looked up at Mitchell, heartbroken. We both stood there motionless, neither of us knowing what to say.

"Did you find her car?" he inquired, barely above a whisper.

"I apologize, sir, but this is the first we've heard about a car. Was this mentioned in the missing person's report that was filed?" I asked, hoping that a huge piece of evidence like that wasn't sitting somewhere getting destroyed.

"Mitchell!" I called his name hoping he had an answer.

"We did file a report but, as of yet, we haven't heard back from anyone on it. The police said that there would be a BOLO (be on the lookout) out for it," he added.

"Just in case you didn't, it is a white, 2022 Lexus IS. All white with a red interior. There is a customized license plate that reads UGA-BALL," Mrs. Seasons specified.

Mitchell immediately radioed in the car's description with an all-points bulletin.

"It seems to me that it's time for you two to leave now, especially since you have some work to do finally," Mr. Seasons rudely spat. "You can see your way out."

At this point, I had no problem leaving and giving the grieving parents time to process. I nodded and made prayer hands toward them before Mitchell and I exited the room. Mrs. Seasons called out to me.

"Detective Lane." She walked over to where we stood. "I can tell that you have a child, or children, by the way you have shown compassion. If you don't do anything else in life, can you at least promise me that you will find the monster that did this to our daughter and bring justice for my sweet Amber? We will offer a reward for any information, and even more if it leads to an arrest," she added.

"I'll make sure that information is put out there, Mrs. Seasons," I told her before parting ways. We made our way over to our vehicle quickly by cutting directly across the grass.

"That was an emotional experience, huh?" Mitchell questioned before unlocking the doors.

"Yeah, it was. It definitely wasn't what I expected. By the way, did you get the envelope with the photos before we left?" I wanted to know, dreading a hike back up the hill to retrieve them if he didn't.

"Of course I did, Lane." Mitchell paused, resting his arms on the roof of the vehicle. He stared back up at the Seasons's residence. I followed his eyes back up the hill, only to notice that there was nothing there. I returned my gaze to him, while he merely remained fixated on the reality stars' home.

"Hey, is everything alright? Do I need to drive?" I asked, not understanding his sudden daydreaming spell.

Mitchell shook his head back and forth as if he was literally shaking thoughts out of his head. "I'm fine, Lane. You know that bad feeling that you were telling me about earlier?"

"I do. And…?" I responded quickly.

"Well, that now makes the both of us with one."

CHAPTER TEN

MISSY

"Where-where am I?" Carla mumbled, slowly regaining consciousness. Carla groaned and shifted, a look of horror on her face. I knew then that she had realized she had been violated. I watched her struggle to free herself through the camera. Mister stood in the shadows, out of her view, awaiting my instructions.

I was sure that her nostrils still had residuals from the chemical used to sedate her that caused her to cough. She struggled to bring her hands to cover her mouth as the restraints did their job. She would soon realize that the more she struggled, the tighter they would get. She was becoming more irate. The last thing we needed was for her to bruise herself and mess up our plans.

"Hey-hey, you need to relax, you don't want to hurt yourself. The more you move, the worse it will get," I warned her over a microphone. "You are very weak, and those restraints are for your safety," I advised her, as I tried to get her to calm herself.

"Fuck that and fuck you, you bitch! LET ME OUT OF HERE!" Carla screamed at the top of her lungs.

I knew at that very instant that she would need another sedative. I turned on the floodlights that illuminated the area Carla was being housed in, giving her the spotlight she deserved. By the time she realized that someone was in the room with her, Mister had his hand around her neck. "Didn't she tell you to calm down?!" Mister wasted no time in applying more pressure as he spoke.

I knew I had to get down to the room before he killed her. "Hey-hey! Let go of her. Let. Her. Go, Now! Are you fucking crazy?" Mister was looking at me dumbfounded. "No bruises or marks remember, or we'll have to toss her?" I reiterated how things needed to be.

Mister relinquished his grip on the woman's neck, then he pushed her away, causing her to fall over on her side. The woman did her best to catch her breath. Her eyes met mine as I approached her. I could tell that she recognized me, and I could feel her fear.

"How are you doing, young lady? You don't look so good. See, I told you to relax, that it was for your safety, but your generation is a rebellious bunch." I helped her sit up properly, then I took a seat on the stool in front of her. "There we go…is that better? You have to excuse my friend, he can be extremely rude at times with our guests, especially when he sees someone being so ungrateful, such as how you were moments ago."

The young woman surprised me with what she said next. "Ungrateful? You sick fucks have some nerves! I tried to help your pitiful ass, and this is how you fucking repay me?! Let me out of here now, you fucking bitch!" Carla yelled before lunging at me, using her head as a weapon. Her attempt was unexpected, and she caught me square on my nose. Water immediately formed in my eyes as the blood began to flow freely out of my nose.

"You fucking bitch…I oughta kill your stupid ass!" I was pissed and embarrassed. I held my shirt up to my face to stop the blood flow.

Without being instructed to, Mister rushed over and with one swift motion, he had his hand around Carla's throat again. "You little bitch, you're lucky I don't slit your fucking throat right now!" Mister declared vehemently while still holding her by her neck with little force.

I was still a little dazed, but the blood flow from my nose had slowed down. I let my shirt fall and let the slow trickle of blood go down my face and over my mouth. I could tell by the look on Carla Mango's face that what she saw terrified her. I smiled as I walked over to her once again, a sinister feeling overcoming me.

"You can let her go." I used my hand that was now blood soaked to caress the young woman's face gently, she recoiled at my touch. "What, you don't like blood? You know, Carla, I once had a lot of rage and anger built up in me just like you. I walked around with the notion that the world should operate how I wanted it to. I was so naïve, so gullible Carla, but life has a funny way of giving you its ass to kiss, and waking you up. Would you agree?"

The woman shook her head left to right, not uttering a word. "I mean, look at the situation that you're in now." I paused to let her reflect, as she looked around the room. "Mister, obviously our guest doesn't seem to like how hospitable we have been to her, hopefully we can do something to change that. By the way, I forgive you Carla, you're doing what comes natural, as I am. We'll talk again in the morning. For now, I'm going to let you get your proper rest in hopes that you'll be much more cooperative and grateful that you're still alive," I added

"I don't need to sleep on shiii…" Carla tried to say, but her words were suddenly cut off as Mister's fist slammed into the side of her head. The woman fell over onto her side with a loud thud, causing her shackles to snatch her wrist violently. Mister retrieved the dazed woman who was now slumped over barely conscious, then propped her up against the wall.

"What in the fuck was that, Mister? You do know that it is a female, and not to mention a woman that we need and have waited over a month to get. We have easier ways to knock her out you know… you fucking brute! At the end of the day, she's still a woman!" I couldn't believe what he just did. I wasn't too mad as it was done in my defense.

"I know, but she…" he was frustrated and angry, and I understood. "She's too feisty, and might be a problem, we need to get rid of her." Mister was adamant.

I walked over to where Mister now stood. He was watching me

intently as I approached; his concern evident. I grabbed him by the bottom of his shirt, then I used it to wipe the semi-dried blood covering my nose and mouth. Mister stood still not saying a word. I let go of the now bloody shirt then wrapped my arms around his waist.

I looked up at him with all the seriousness I could muster, then I mouthed words that he knew I would never repeat again. "Don't you ever in your life tell me, or suggest what I or we should do. The last time that I checked, any decision that is to be made, is solely by me. I decide what is best for us, is that understood?" I removed my arms from around his waist.

Mister peered at me, and I could tell he was processing what I said. Although I knew he could break me in two at will, I also knew that he respected me and was well aware that I had his best interest. "The girl will be fine. You did what you thought was right. If you think she's going to be a problem, do what you must to ensure she stays restrained, but she must be sedated," I informed him.

I turned to face the young woman slumped up against the wall like a homeless person trying to sleep, then I glanced back at Mister before I landed a violent kick to the helpless and incapacitated young woman's stomach.

"You fucking bitch, don't you ever put your fucking hands on me! I think I handled that well, Mister." Carla Mango began coughing violently from the unsuspecting blow.

"You just told me not to bruise her, Missy."

He was right, but she needed to be taught a lesson. "She'll be okay, as you can tell by her cough," I told him.

"Is there anything else that you need me to do, besides sedating her again?" Mister asked.

"No, just sedate her for now, and in the morning, I'll check her for any injuries that might cause us to just dispose of her."

"What about the parking lot where we got her from? Do I need to go back?" Mister inquired.

"No. There's no need for you to go back there. Nothing was left to chance with this one." I pointed at our prisoner lying on the floor unconscious. "Carla Mango voluntarily got into our vehicle, we didn't have to use force, so there is no evidence to secure. What I need for you to do is to prepare the other room for when she wakes."

"Can I..." Mister's voice trailed off slowly. "Can I stay with her for a while...I mean, at least before, you know?" he pleaded with me, sounding like a child, desiring to stay with a close friend.

"No, and you know why! You know the rules, do I need to reiterate them? Do not test me, or touch her, while I'm gone... Am I clear?" I hoped that he would listen.

"Yeah, I understand," he grumbled. His disappointment was evident because of his plans being thwarted.

"Good. I'm going to get cleaned up." I cozied up to him once again and let him hold me briefly.

I could see our reflection coming off the mirrored windows and the dried blood looking like small rubies coming out of my nose. I laid my head on his chest, and he held me as if I meant the world to him. It was a feeling I'd never had, and one that I was always thankful to him for providing. I knew that he loved me unconditionally, but I also knew that I would never see him for anything other than what he was: a trained and willing killer.

I ended the embrace, then walked over to where Carla leaned up against the wall. I tried to grab her by her chin, but she began snapping from left to right rapidly.

"Stop, before I slit your fucking throat right here and now," I stated calmly

Carla's eyes opened, and I could see the fear and sadness rolled into one facial expression, worthy of a photo. No amount of training or workout that she had to endure had felt this bad, I was sure of it. All of the fight and will to live that she had previously was now gone. There was no speech that any coach could give her right now that would boost her morale, or her courage. Even with me knowing all these things, I thought I saw a smile or smirk develop on her face.

"Do you find this amusing? If so, I'm glad you found something to smile about, Carla. Let's see if you have that smile on your face in the next few minutes. I'm sure that you think all of this is random, that you just happened to be in the wrong place at the wrong time. That cliche is hardly ever the case; people get what they deserve, one way or another. Continuing on, you, young lady, are the only child born to William and Diane Mango."

Carla remained quiet and emotionless as I continued to recite her and her family's bio. "Your father is an investment banker, and your mother is a shitty accountant, to say the least, albeit very successful. They have a nice ranch style home in Fayetteville, North Carolina. I can't understand why you guys have so many cats. How am I doing?"

I paused to gauge her reaction from the information I just told her. Her face was indifferent, as if she didn't care. "I'm not trying to talk your head off Carla, I just wanted you to know that this was not some random abduction. Have you ever noticed how much you can learn about a person through social media? Like, for instance, where they like to eat, who their family members are, and in some cases, their exact location when they are out enjoying themselves. You, my dear Carla, did all three.

"You talked about your family coming to town on social media, and also how you couldn't wait to go to Zumba class. It didn't take long to figure out which one you'd be attending. I mean, a rich girl like yourself had to go to where the best instructors were. I'm thankful that I don't have mindless kids running around in this dangerous world, exposing themselves to the evils that be."

I could tell that the young woman was now starting to fathom all the possibilities of bodily harm that might befall her and her loved ones. She looked hopeless and helpless, just like I wanted her to feel. The tears that formed in her eyes let me know that every thought that I had was spot on.

"It looks like someone is ready to cooperate, and enjoy the time she has left on this earth. Whether you know it or not, those tears bring out your eyes, literally. I never understood how a beautiful young woman, like yourself, wasted your time playing a men's sport. Oh, you like women, don't you? That's it. Was that your girlfriend that you were working out with, huh? She was cute, if it was." Carla remained silent.

"Please, I'm begging you to let me go home. What…whatever you think I've done or that my family may have done, I'm sorry. I truly am.

I-I just want to go home to my family," she gave a heartfelt appeal that fell on deaf ears as tears finally exploded from her eyes.

Mister and I exchanged looks at her comment. "OMG. To be honest, Carla, I'm totally disappointed in you. The tough girl act was really working like a charm on me. As you see, I didn't punish you like I could've for head butting me because you had gained my respect. You are actually the first person that has tried that to my surprise, and it's been a good experience, but never again though after today. I want you to know that before you leave this earth, you and people like you, will understand that your money, status, and who you know will not help you. Do you have anything to say now?"

Carla shook her head from left to right, not knowing how to answer. "You don't look elite anymore. You're not that superstar athlete that everyone had great expectations for, now are you?" I questioned, not really looking for an answer. "Get her into 'The Room' so that we can show Carla our hospitality."

Mister's eyes lit up after hearing that he was to take her to 'The Room', while Carla cringed as the oddity of a man made his way towards her. As his face came into full view, she could see that he now had on a hood that draped over his face. The horror on her face when he pulled his hood off was priceless. Carla tested out our sound proof walls as her screams resonated off the mirrored walls. They intensified while Mister pulled out the syringe and inserted it into her arm. Carla's body became limp within seconds.

"There you go…get you some rest, Carla. It will all be over with real soon," I let her know.

CHAPTER ELEVEN
DETECTIVE LANE

I woke up feeling rejuvenated as I had slept double-digit hours. I had been smiling and laughing non stop since June arrived, my daughter was always a welcome entity. Neither of us realized just how much we'd missed each other. Sure, we spoke every day, but the intimacy of having your child in your presence is irreplaceable, especially for a healthy relationship.

Whether June knew it or not, her company was exactly what I needed to feel some semblance of normalcy, especially with everything going on now. I looked at the clock and sat at the end of the bed imitating Mister Rogers as I put on my shoes and holster. June entered my room.

"Hey, Mom. Are you on your way out?" She floated over to where I sat then kissed me on my forehead. The smile I wore grew even bigger.

"What was that for?"

"For being such a good mom, of course. Do I need a reason to plant a kiss on you?" she quipped.

"You don't, and yes, I'm headed into the office now to meet Mitchell as soon as I finish getting dressed. Why are you up so early,

June? I thought spring break meant sleeping in and relaxing, at least that's how it was for us."

"Well, it doesn't mean that to our generation. While the next person is sleeping or resting, someone the same age is getting rich or doing something positive; I'm trying to do both. I have to get out and get it, Mom. It's really that simple."

"You're right, things have changed."

"I'm going to meet Rayven at the gym around eight." She looked at me with a look that let me know she wanted to talk about something.

"It's written all over your face, you don't have to say a word," I sang. "What's going on? I do have enough time to talk, if you need to." I wanted her to know that she was important.

She came right out with it, and it wasn't what I was expecting. "I am thinking of playing basketball next season. I spoke to the coach and have already had my physical done. The shoulder injury that I sustained my senior year has since healed. The team doctors, of course, will ensure I'm good. My injury didn't require surgery, remember?"

"The gym…and basketball, are you serious, June?"

"Yes, Mom, I am, and don't let me find out you are mixed with a parrot, you're always repeating mine, or someone else's statement."

"First off, I do that to gain clarification. Yes, I've started trying to get my stamina right and tone up my body, just in case I make the team as a walk-on. I mean, I couldn't stay cute and chubby my whole life," she jokingly stated as she sat down next to me.

"Well, I guess if you're healthy enough to try out, then why not; you are a good point guard. I'm sure that you'll find a way to balance basketball with academics, because if not, I can assure you that they just don't give out those engineering degrees. Also, be extra careful while home for spring break, there's a lot going on. As a matter of fact, I think it would be pretty cool if you invited a few friends over and hung out here," I suggested, loosely encouraging the gathering.

June angled her head in my direction and placed her hand on my shoulder, a gesture I used to do to her when she was fighting a lost cause.

"Mom, please don't take this the wrong way, but I'm your daughter. Your daughter, let me reiterate that, once again. I have mimicked everything I have seen you do since birth…figuratively, of course."

"I'm glad you clarified, figuratively."

"Of course, Mom. I see you got jokes though, you're hilarious. But anyway, before I lose my train of thought, what makes you all paranoid, or should I say overprotective? Whatever you have going on at work, please don't project that negative energy on me. See, what you don't know is that I'm actually trying to be in these Atlanta streets enjoying myself, like every other normal teenager who doesn't have a homicide detective as a mother. Like you used to say when I'd ask you about your job, your favorite line used to be, and I quote, 'June, the less you know, the better off you are.' That was cut and dry, so I stopped asking."

My smile quickly turned into a smirk that would only suffice for an elementary school picture. "You're absolutely right, young lady." I stood up, walked over to my vanity dresser, took a seat, and began applying makeup.

"Mom, tell me you're not throwing a silent temper tantrum. I see what's happening here, but before you tune me out, let me say this. My lovely mother, as usual, I trust that whatever case you are working on, you and Mitchell can handle it. I also need you to trust that what you have taught me, along with the weapon that you bought me, is enough to keep me safe. Now, if you don't mind, I'm about to head to the gym, then continue to enjoy my spring break without any trepidation whatsoever, as you taught me to do."

I peered at her through the vanity mirror. Her long, straight hair was tied loosely and hung over her left shoulder, giving off a "Look how pretty I am, but I'm here to workout" vibe. I studied her features that reminded me so much of my mother, then I quickly noticed that she had some sort of tattoo on her neck.

"When did you decide to mark your body up with some crazy artwork? Are you serious, June? I guess college life has truly kicked in for someone, huh?"

"Really, Mom? I'm trying to figure out if that was just a random statement, or were you asking a question. It doesn't matter… This crazy artwork that you are referring to, is a Japanese tattoo of your name." She leaned over and gave me a kiss on the top of my head. "I will pick us up something to eat for dinner, my treat, of course."

"As much as I hate to admit it, June, you are so much like your father. You have a way of mimicking things that people do to you as a calming or loving gesture. The only thing that I hope, when it comes to you, is that you don't use it as a form of manipulation, as he did."

"And on that note, Mom, I'm out. I'll talk to you later," she playfully joked, exiting my room before I could reply. I shook my head thinking about the daughter I now had versus the daughter I drove down to Savannah State a year ago. With her newfound maturity, her womanly transformation, and now armed with a good sense of humor, June was going to make some guy very lucky someday.

I heard the sound of a notification on my phone, signaling that June had exited the house. I did a quick double check in the mirror, then checked around the room to ensure I had everything I needed before heading out the door.

I arrived at the precinct at 8:15 a.m. and immediately, a chilling feeling came over me. To my surprise, no one was milling around, so I headed directly to my desk without having to say good morning, a rarity.

"You finally made it, huh?" Mitchell's voice came out of nowhere, startling me.

"Just got here. Where is everyone?" I inquired, as I observed all the empty desks.

"Some are in training and the rest are in a meeting with the Captain," he answered, before he took a seat across from me at his desk. We stared at each other momentarily before trying to speak at the same time.

"Go ahead, you first Lane," he suggested, then leaned back in his chair.

"Thank you, I appreciate it. I know we've just started this case, but something seems off. I can't put my finger on it, but I don't think this was random."

Mitchell sat up straight in his chair, then leaned forward to where only I could hear him, although we were the only occupants in the room; force of habit, I'm sure.

"The only suspicion that I had came from the groundskeeper, but even that notion went out of my head after speaking with the Seasons, which was a moment in itself. I didn't see anything out of place, at least not with them."

"Well, I sense something, and my senses don't just kick in. I'm like Spiderman in that regard. I have a feeling that Amber might not have been the squeaky-clean daughter they make her out to be, but that doesn't matter. What matters is that we stop whoever it is that is trying to disrupt life in our city." I was concerned.

"Her parents are basically saints to her. The medical assistant gave us a rundown on how much she was loved. She told us that she watched the Seasons' daughter grow up on TV, along with them. How sneaky could she have been? Oh, and let us not forget that she was a star athlete, which means that she was always in the spotlight…never alone too much," he pushed for added measure.

"Okay, Mitchell… Then explain the good doctor's face when she saw her daughter's gym bag still in the closet after saying she was headed to workout. Pass me the file, please." Mitchell handed me the file, then walked around and sat on the edge of my desk.

"I have some sticky notes attached to things that jumped out at me," he advised.

I read over the notes that were placed on the file then removed one of the graphic photos. I focused on the small mark on her face that was no longer covered by makeup. Her autopsy made no mention of this blemish, but I did.

"Mitchell, here, take a look at the mark directly under her left eye, and tell me what you think that is or from." I handed him the photo, and he stood up and held it up to the light. "It almost looks like a teardrop."

"Bingo, that's exactly what I came up with." Mitchell held the photo up towards the light again, ignoring my sarcasm earlier.

"Now it looks like a birthmark of something. It doesn't look tattooed," he changed his reply, indecisive as usual.

"It's not a birthmark," I assured him as I showed him the cutout photo from her school yearbook.

"Okay, so what do you think it is, Lane?" he asked, as if he had an answer.

"I'm not sure, but here's a key piece of information that you don't have notated, Mitchell." I pointed out as I held my finger up to where he could see them. He read them aloud.

"Vaginal and anal penetration… Sheesh! This is giving me a sick feeling now. I guess after reading 'no DNA available,' I missed it. Wait… Didn't the Seasons say that her boyfriend was on a trip out of the country with his family?"

"They did state that, but what if he wasn't? We know that there was no trace of semen, hair follicles, or prints recovered," I stated matter of factly.

"I think we might need to speak to her parents again. What do you think?" Mitchell recommended.

"At this point, that would be moot. What would we possibly ask them about that we hadn't already? Going in there…telling them that we have evidence that their daughter had sex in both orifices might not go too well," I countered.

"Indeed. I think about the way her body was displayed and positioned, which leads me to believe that maybe he could have been close with our victim. It would explain why there are no contusions or signs of a struggle other than that odd mark on her face. The report says she died as a result of asphyxiation. I would think she'd be a fighter, a natural reflex for an athlete."

I dissected Mitchell's last sentence. I found it strange now that I thought about it. Where was the fight from a young college athlete in the position she was in, I pondered. There should have at least been some kind of defense wound notated, but there wasn't. Here was a young woman who was missing for four days before her body was discovered, and from the evidence, not one time did she put up a fight?

"Mitchell, when you think about it, this woman doesn't have any defense wounds or scars notated. I'm thinking that she may have been drugged." I shifted the photos on my desk until I found the one I was looking for. The one that showed the up-close visual of her face. "I've been thinking about this mark under her left eye again." I was interrupted by Mitchell's desk phone ringing.

"Let me get that," he commented, before walking around to his desk. I watched his facial expression change to a look of surprise. "We have to go," he notified me and retrieved his note pad off of his desk.

"What's going on? Go where?" I probed as I stood up, knowing that I'd be going wherever he was going at this point.

"That was the sergeant at the desk notifying me that the Seasons are down the hall in the interview room waiting on us."

"For what? Did you ask them to come here?" I asked with a stern look.

"Of course not, but we need to get in there. This ought to be very interesting," he said, leading the way.

———

We walked into Interview Room One, and I expected to see Mrs. Seasons, but not the young man that accompanied her. His hair was a sandy blond with dark highlights. He kept his eyes glued to the floor with his hands clasped together tightly. I sat across from the pair, while Mitchell took up a post near the two-way mirror behind me.

"Nice to see you Mrs. Seasons, and…" I used my head and eyes to gesture to the young man sitting beside her.

"Dexter. His name is Dexter," she clarified.

"Dexter, is there something wrong? Can he not speak for himself?" I wanted to know, maybe he had a disability. My statement caused the young man to finally take his eyes off of the floor. He gave me a piercing look, before speaking.

"If your boyfriend or girlfriend, and childhood friend, were murdered, how would you be looking or feeling?" he calmly expressed.

I had to agree with his logic. Everyone expressed themselves differently, but at this moment, his grief was not my concern.

"Mrs. Seasons, this is a pleasant surprise, but may I ask where Mr. Seasons is?

"He won't be joining us," she dryly replied.

"That's too bad. Well, if you're here, I'm sure there is a good reason for you and Dexter to visit this morning."

Her posture stiffened, and her chin rose slightly. "I brought Dexter here to clear his name, and prevent any negative press that might include him. Ever since he came home from his trip, he has been harassed and made out to be a-a…I can't even say it. People are threatening him by saying things like 'it's always the boyfriend.' I know for a fact that Dexter isn't capable of such a thing."

"Mrs. Seasons, after hearing your reasoning for coming, I must tell you that there was no reason for you or Dexter to come and clear his name. We already verified his alibi."

"Really? I wanted to come though," Dexter spoke again, barely above a whisper.

"What did you say?" Mitchell questioned, moving from the two-way mirror closer to Dexter.

"Look, I've been receiving calls and texts from people I never gave my number to. I had nothing to do with Amber's murder, and I'm glad you know that, but no one out there knows that it seems. I first met Amber when she was six years old at a mutual friend's birthday party. We grew to be best friends, then eventually lovers. I loved her more than anything in the world; we were planning on getting married one day." A wave of emotion came over him, and he began to shed tears. Mrs. Seasons seized his hand in an effort to comfort him.

"Was it because she was pregnant?" Mitchell blurted out, almost causing me to tell him to get out.

"Pregnant!? No, why would you ask that question?" He seemed surprised by the implication.

"Dexter, it seems that you weren't aware that Amber was pregnant?

I would think that the potential father, the childhood friend and lover, would be privy to that information, unless you weren't the father. But, it's moot at this point because being the best friend you would've still known. According to the medical examiner, Amber Seasons had an abortion last month," Mitchell rudely added.

I watched Mrs. Seasons' face contort to a look of disconcert, as if she had in fact heard the news of a pregnancy and abortion before now. If she was already aware, then why wasn't Dexter?

"Hand me her file, Mitchell." I flipped through a few pages for dramatic fashion before reading the exact date of her termination.

"Okay officer, okay… You're right, Amber was pregnant." The way he said it, though, sounded as if he disagreed with the decision to terminate. I looked at Mrs. Seasons, and the expression that she now wore confirmed that it may have been her idea. Dexter looked at Mrs. Seasons for an answer, and true to her reality television performances, didn't disappoint.

"Yes, what you have disclosed is true, or was, about Amber being pregnant. We thought it best if she didn't go full term, which was the right decision. As you know, she had a lot to look forward to in life and having a child as a freshman in college wouldn't have been the best decision."

Everyone in the room was looking at her in disbelief. She had taken it upon herself to decide for her daughter, and Dexter.

"Mrs. Seasons…"

"That's Doctor," she spat, cutting Mitchell off.

"Doctor," he responded, clearly becoming fed up with her reality star antics. "You use the word 'we' when you speak of making that decision. Dexter, were you involved in this decision?"

"Of course he agreed!" she interjected, clearly flustered.

"He wasn't asking you, Mrs. Seasons… I mean Doctor," I conferred, as I defended my partner from her disrespect earlier. "Just so you know, your input to terminate what would have been your grand-child, a grandchild that would be here when your daughter isn't, is something you will have to live with, not Dexter."

Dexter jumped out of his seat to where he was now standing over

Mrs. Seasons and looking down on her. "No, no, no, I didn't agree. I never agreed to any of it!" His blood was boiling. Mitchell walked over and placed a hand on his shoulder.

"Have a seat, Dexter," Mitchell stated as he gently grabbed the young man's arm. He did as he was told.

"How did the Seasons and Amber making the decision to terminate her pregnancy without your consent make you feel? Did you get angry?" I probed.

Dexter was perplexed. His look was as if I had said something offensive. "I see what you're doing. I was out of town with my family when Amber was killed."

"You were, but since when did that stop a plan from going into action? I'm aware that you could have just as easily paid someone. It would have been understandable to have a thought like that, being that she took your unborn child away from you." I played my card to see what kind of reaction I would get.

"Is this an interrogation? Because if it is, I think I may need to call my lawyer. I brought Dexter here on the assumption that he might share something that could help you find my deceased daughter's killer, not for him to be berated like he's a suspect," Mrs. Seasons conveyed.

"I truly apologize if I offended you, Dr. Seasons. I'm only doing my job, which is to take emotions out of the equation. I have witnessed killers walk in here under their own accord and claim innocence, only to get caught committing the same crime a week later. I apologize to you as well, Dexter. I know that this is tough, and no, this is not an interrogation. If you don't mind continuing, I have a few more questions," I apologized genuinely.

"I'm not the bad guy here," Dexter declared, looking Mitchell in his eyes.

"No one said you were. Continue, please," Mitchell let it be known.

"Well, Amber did call me the night of her disappearance." He paused briefly as memories of his late girlfriend surfaced. "She called me and told me that she would be going to the sporting goods store to buy a new gym bag."

"Explains why her gym bag was left in the closet when she said she was going to work out," Mitchell stated. Mrs. Seasons' face registered relief as she now knew her daughter had not deceived them with her whereabouts the night of her disappearance.

"What store did she go to?" she interrupted.

"Dr. Seasons, can you please let me or Mitchell do all the questioning, if you don't mind? Thank you," I told her not wanting to miss anything with her interruptions.

"GameChangers Sporting Goods," he replied, trying to catch the tears that escaped his eyes. "She has an account there."

I looked over at Mitchell, and without saying a word, he knew what I wanted. "I'm on it now, Lane," he said, before exiting the interview room.

"Thank you for that, Dexter." When the door closed, I returned to my focus on the broken young man in front of me and the distraught reality star that accompanied him.

I felt empathy for both; their road to making peace with this tragedy would probably be long and hard. Dexter had been robbed of the decision to father a child and the right to enjoy life with the woman he loved, and Helen Seasons missed the chance to see her daughter conquer the goals she set out to accomplish. I did my best to formulate the right words to comfort them both.

"Dr. Seasons… Dexter." I made eye contact with them both as I said each their names. "I truly am sorry for your loss. I can assure you that my partner and I will do everything we can to bring a positive outcome for you. I ask you to be patient, and if you have any information that you think to be useful, please feel free to contact me."

"I appreciate that detective, thank you. This has been one of the hardest things I have ever had to deal with and accept in my entire life. I pray that you find justice for my daughter before someone else is sitting where I am, feeling torn apart." Her eyes were full of tears. She wiped them as best she could before standing up. Dexter stood up as well, then intertwined his arm into Helen Seasons' then walked over to the door.

"Please." He nodded to the door.

"Of course, excuse me." I walked over to the door, knocked twice, and immediately the door was opened.

"Thank you for coming down. Please drive safely, it's wet out there."

"Thank you, and we will," Dexter replied, escorting Mrs. Seasons out the door. I left the room shortly after gathering our things. I made it back to my desk where Mitchell was scribbling in his notepad. He stood quickly and grabbed his keys off the desk. "I got the address, let's roll," he ordered. I locked the Seasons' file in my desk and followed him out of the precinct.

CHAPTER TWELVE

MISSY

"Don't worry, I'll be back in a few days. You know why I had to come out here, so relax and stay inside. I have to go, we're about to take off, and I need some rest. I will call you later tonight," I told Mister, hoping that he'd follow my instructions. He had a habit of straying when he felt cooped up due to his PTSD.

"But…ok then," Mister reluctantly accepted my decision before disconnecting the call. After we hung up, I closed my eyes to try to get some rest. It has been nonstop work, and I was mentally exhausted. Coming to California always made me think of my dad, and the last time I saw him. My very existence is owed to my dad, as he brought the monster he needed to see out of me with his last conversation. *"Cathy, I don't know if I'll ever get out of here, and I don't know if I want to. This place has taken a real toll on your mom and I."*

"Why would you say that, Daddy? Mom and I both know that you didn't do anything wrong."

"My little princess, you know you will always be our Lil' Missy. You were always wise beyond your years, which is why your mom and I called you that. I love you so much. I know you know that."

"I love you too, Daddy."

"It's time you know the truth, Cathy. And the truth of the matter is that I destroyed our family. I'm locked away from all of the people that I love right now because of it."

"What do you mean? What are you talking about Dad?"

"See, Cathy, although I didn't do what I'm accused of, I am guilty of ruining my marriage. I should have never let myself be manipulated by those people. The reason you need to know this is because your mother is no longer here for me to finally be honest with her."

Dad closed his eyes looking like he was ready to tell me something that transpired from that life altering day. A day that had haunted him over and over. "I'm about to tell you some things that will change how you see me, but you need to know the truth. Don't interrupt me, Missy, just listen." Dad proceeded to tell me the graphic details that had led to him being incarcerated.

"The day started off as a normal day for me. I made my rounds around the campus, according to my repair list. I loved working at the campus, I didn't have anyone looking over my shoulder while I worked. I'd been working at UCLA for a few years at that time, fixing everything from air conditioners to bathroom toilets. It was the perfect job, as it wasn't far from our house, or your school. I had a love for sports...any kind of sport, so I spent a lot of time in the athletic department engaging with the athletes and coaches. I made sure that they never had any problems that existed longer than a few days. Because of the way I was willing to help and do things outside of my job duties, I became well liked. They gave me tickets to the softball and volleyball games that I would take you to. I knew when I took the job there that UCLA was a hotbed for young, spoiled rotten kids that flaunted their status as well as their bodies without any qualms."

"What does that mean, Dad?"

"It is where people think they are better than another person based on several factors, mainly race and financial status. Your mom advised me not to take that job, with the fear of me possibly being put in a situation to be tempted by offers from young women and sometimes young men."

"Dad!"

"No, never. I will admit that as a man I found several of the girls that went to school there attractive, but I never crossed the line by saying anything inappropriate, nor did I accept any gifts. There was this one girl, her name was Racheal. She was a star softball player who always spoke to me and gave me a smile when we passed each other. As I told you when I started, I want you to know the truth. She was the only person that I would go out of my way to make sure we crossed paths on most days, not because I was interested in her, but because of the way she treated me compared to everyone else.

One day I was on my way to the athletic building, and I saw Racheal and her friends sitting on the lawn relaxing just enjoying the sun as they usually do. Racheal and I made eye contact with each other, and I smiled, but she didn't. She simply nodded, then lowered her head. I don't know what made me approach them, but I did. I can remember the conversation like it was yesterday. I walked up and said. 'Hi, nice day out here. Hope you guys have a great day.' No one spoke back, as they gave me looks of disdain, as I hovered over them in my stained uniform."

"'Um, like, excuse you, you're blocking what makes this a good day, in the sun, by standing there. The maintenance building is that way,' one of the guys had said to me.

'Like, dude, you're blocking the sun. Didn't you hear him, you jerk?' another one had said."

"'Yeah, like we don't need anything fixed over here, perv!'"

"I was in disbelief and embarrassed. I immediately looked at Racheal for any attempt to come to my defense, being that these were her friends. Although we didn't know each other personally, I felt that she had enough respect for me not to allow it to happen, or intervene. She acted as if she didn't know me, and joined in with her friends as they laughed at my expense. She had no regard for feelings.

I did my best to act as if the incident didn't bother me, and I forced a smile before walking away. I was embarrassed, but above all, I was pissed off."

"I continued to work around the campus, doing my best to avoid all the paths that students would take as I did my rounds. Later on that

day, while on my way back to the maintenance building, I saw Racheal standing alone by a tree looking in my direction. I quickly turned in the opposite direction, doing my best to avoid any type of confrontation in public there. I needed that job, but she followed me."

"'Hey... Hey, mister! Hey, hold up, please' I heard her call out. I continued to head to the office until I felt a small hand grip my shoulder.

"'Hey, I know that you heard me calling you. Look, you have every right to not want to talk to me,'" Racheal had stated then followed it up with her captivating smile.

"With that statement, and her smile, I decided to listen to what she had to say."

"But why, Dad?"

"I don't know why, and that's why I'm here talking to you now. I guess I just wanted to know why she acted the way she did."

"'I just want to apologize for my friend's behavior earlier. I need you to know that's not a true reflection of me. As you know, I'm an athlete and with that, sometimes we become part of the cheering section, being that we're never there. I was wrong by not speaking up, and I admit that. They're actually some cool friends, but they can be awful at times.'"

"I'm sure," I replied back to her sarcastically, truly just wanting the conversation to end.

"I know you're upset, and you have every right to be. I should've said something, but..."

"Look, even as we talk now, I realize that you don't even know my name. Not to mention, who wants to be cool with a maintenance man, right? I have things to do Racheal, so take care."

"No, that's not what I was about to say, and don't try to dismiss me like that. I'm trying to genuinely apologize. There has to be something that I can do to make up for it...maybe if I gave you some cash?"

"I accept your apology, but I'm a grown man, and not someone that can be bought. To be honest, I don't think there's anything that can make up for the blatant disrespect that most of you rich, spoiled, and self entitled kids possess. It might not be your fault as most behavior is

hereditary. I wish you the best, Racheal," I told her then walked into the office. The office was empty, I poured myself a cup of coffee, and before I could sit down, I heard the creaking of the maintenance room door as it opened slowly, and it was Racheal.

"Racheal what-what are you doing here?" I demanded, but she ignored my questioning and slowly began to unbutton her shirt.

"Before I knew it, I was doing things that I shouldn't have done. My boss walked in and caught us in the act. Racheal grabbed her things and acted as if I had violated her, and my boss didn't hesitate to take her side. The campus police were called and from that day forward I was taken out of you and your Mom's lives.

"How could you let that happen, Dad?" I remember being so angry.

"I-I don't know. It just happened. It wasn't supposed to happen, I just..." was all he could say.

We cried together as my dad began to give me instructions that I would live by for the rest of my life. I listened to each and every word that he told me with all of the concentration that I could muster at that age.

"Cathy, this will probably be the last time that you will be visiting me. I need you to accept that I am responsible for your mom's depressive state of mind that caused her to commit suicide. I lied, I cheated, and most importantly, I left you out there alone with people that will never love you like I do."

"No, Daddy, that's not true. Momma was sick, and they..."

"Damnit, Catherine Raisery! Now, you listen to me. In life, you have to realize that people are going to disappoint you, no matter how much you think they won't. I'm a disappointment, and I'm trying to make sure that you won't be. You need to know that people will only show you the side of them that they want you to see, and after that, it's up to you to determine if it's the real them. What I'm saying doesn't make sense right now, but in time you will see that it does.

As I continued to cry, I watched my father's facial expression change to one that I'd never witnessed. He began to laugh, and I didn't know why.

"That's right, cry, because after today, I don't want you to ever shed another tear."

I wiped my face, and my tears began to subside.

"Do you know how pathetic you look right now? I need you to be strong and control your emotions no matter the situation. Do you know that the people that helped put me in here, the rich and entitled, would love to see me cry, wallowing in self pity? Never would I give them that satisfaction, and neither will you. Now you wipe away those tears of self pity and hold your head up. I need you to remember this, Missy, the next time that someone makes you cry, you better make sure that someone else will be crying as well. Never cry alone, Catherine Raisery. Do you understand? You make an example out of anyone that tries to." My dad demanded.

"Catherine…Catherine, wake up we are here," the flight attendant announced.

"We are?" Wow, I needed that rest." I stirred from my brief nap, retrieved my phone out of my purse, then typed a text message.

CHAPTER THIRTEEN

MISSY

The door to the charter plane opened inviting thousands of rays of sunlight to flood the plane. I donned my overly large designer shades, checked my appearance, then walked to the door. I peered down at the old frail woman standing at the bottom of the steps, then at the woman standing next to her with the oversized shades and umbrella. A huge smile formed on my face. I walked down and greeted them both with a huge hug.

"How was your trip, Catherine?" The woman who adopted me and changed my life greeted me with a hug.

"It was okay. The food wasn't prepared right the first time, and I had them do it over, but overall the flight from Columbus went well. How are you, Daphne? I'm surprised to see you here." Daphne was not one to frequent anything that had to do with family.

"Why wouldn't I be here?"

"I mean, you are usually out of the country doing whatever it is you do, which is always more important… What do you do anyway?" I quipped

"Mind my business… I am here, Catherine, and that's all that matters at this point. Why you are here is the real question," Daphne stated, throwing one of the many darts she kept for me when we were in the same room, which happened to come out earlier than expected.

"My Grandpa was just as important to me as he was to you, if not more, and you know that."

"Girls…please not right now. Catherine, we need to get going. You and Daphne can catch up later, but please, not in front of the guests with the antics. We have dinner scheduled at 7pm. That should give you two enough time to rest up, and hopefully clear your heads. Wilson, dear, go get their bags." Gramma Ruby ordered the driver that was standing by patiently awaiting orders.

Wilson trekked up the steps of the private plane and met the stewardess, who held two medium-sized bags that he collected, then placed them in the trunk.

"It's okay, Gramma, Catherine and I actually do have a lot of catching up to do. You know we wouldn't dare disrespect the family with our petty quarrels. I do have to get this out though, Catherine. Where do you get the nerve to ask what I do for a living, when no one knows what you do for a living, besides living off of the proceeds of Gramma Ruby and Grandpa's allowance that they give us monthly. I never depended on no one."

"That's enough, Daphne. I said stop it, and dammit, I mean it. You both benefit from our wealth, and neither I, nor your grandpa, cared about it. Unfortunately for Catherine, she didn't have the upbringing you had. Now is not the time for discussing this, and until we lay Pa to rest, I will hear nothing more, before both of you are cut off… Is that understood?" I nodded, and Daphne reluctantly nodded in agreement as well. "Now, get in the car before we get stuck in that god-forsaken traffic."

The feeling of being back in California had me feeling exuberant. It had been months since I had been on the west coast. I was back in the state that I could be free to live, enjoy my wealth, and not have to hide my identity. Since taking up residence in Atlanta with Mister, we had been forced to live as recluses due to our activities.

My place in Georgia was buried deep within the rural industrial area, secluded from all humans, with state of the art everything. I had to compensate for the lack of human interactions that were not allowed for Mister's sake.

Being financially set for life came at a steep price that unfortunately my parents paid with their respective deaths, which sent me into foster care. I struggled with the first two families that I was sent to, and they immediately noticed I had behavioral issues. I was placed back in foster care for re-evaluation, and deemed not fit for community residency.

Adoption was rare once a child reached their teens, and I was only months away from being in the percentile that stayed a ward of the state until legal adulthood if not adopted.

I endured countless hours of therapy, for behavioral problems no one could diagnose. I was labeled as angry, combative, and a rejector of authority; all true. I had every right to be. My anger issues stemmed from the deep-rooted hatred of having my mother and father taken away from me by the people responsible.

I was scheduled to be sent to a group home for troubled teens the upcoming Tuesday. On that Saturday, we hosted a car wash to raise money for a vacation that I wouldn't be going on, but I still chose to participate. As I cleaned cars and collected the proceeds, I never would have imagined that it would set up a chance encounter with my future parents.

The woman that would come to love me more than anyone in the world, besides my parents, spoke to me so kindly upon meeting me. We spoke briefly, and she asked me if I wanted to have a chance at a better life, and I immediately answered, yes. It turned out to be the best decision of my life, as Gramma Ruby, what she told me to call her, had unlimited means of money. I knew the only thing that was left for me to do was exactly as my father had instructed, which was to, "Never Cry Alone." I have kept my promise.

I'm here, can't wait to get back tho. Have big plans. LOL!

CHAPTER FOURTEEN

DETECTIVE LANE

"Hi, Mellissa," I read the cashier's name tag while producing my badge. "Is the manager in?"

Showing her my badge was the equivalent of a shopping receipt. "Can I help you with something?" she inquired with a professional business look.

"Yes, you can page your supervisor, or go get them," I responded back. The baby-faced attendant briefly looked at me, confused, before retrieving the phone and speaking. Her eyes remained glued to mine as she spoke in a low voice.

"He will be here shortly. Is he in trouble?" she pried further, piquing my curiosity.

"Why would he be?" I countered.

She was suddenly at a loss for words, and rightfully so. A tall and slender man wearing a warehouse safety vest approached us. He extended his hand, then introduced himself.

"Hi, I'm the manager, Mark. Is there something that I can do for you?" We both shook his hand.

"My name is Detective Lane, and this is Detective Mitchell. We'd like to speak to you somewhere in private if that's not an inconvenience."

"No, no…of course. Mel, hold it down while I'm gone," he told the young attendant that looked to be no more than twenty years old.

He led us over to a workstation that sat off to the side of the store. From this location, they had a great view of the main walking aisles. "Where's the room you have your security monitoring system set up in?" I asked.

"My what? Security system? Why do you need to see that? Exactly what kind of detectives are you guys?" he questioned, stopping in his tracks. You're not with theft and loss prevention?"

Mitchell chuckled before responding. "Loss prevention is a nice way to put it, but no, we're homicide, sir," Mitchell answered simply.

"Homicide? What is going on?"

"Take us to the security room, and we'll explain everything, Mark." I looked over my shoulder and noticed inquisitive shoppers within earshot. "It's best if we talk when we get in your security room." I gestured by nodding my head in the direction of the GameChangers' customers looking in our direction.

"Yes, of course," he agreed, then led us down a short hallway to a door that sat to the rear with the word **SECURITY** written in large, bold, red, and blue letters.

Mark knocked on the door three times rapidly, I'm sure in a way they weren't used to. A series of locks were heard clicking before the door opened slowly. A large, burly man, with a short cropped beard, opened the door. He wore civilian clothes.

"This is our Loss Prevention Officer, Carlton, and sitting at the monitor is Jake, our Security Analyst. Whatever you need to discuss, you can do so in front of them." Jake turned away from the monitor to face us after hearing his boss's last statement.

"I am Homicide Detective Lane, and this is my partner Detective Mitchell. We are investigating the disappearance of a young woman by the name of Amber Seasons whose last known location was at your store. We've already verified through her account statements that she was here June 9th, to purchase a gym bag and running shoes at eight forty-six p.m. We need you to pull up the footage for that date and hours surrounding her disappearance," I advised, hoping that this wasn't the type of store that deleted footage every twenty-four hours.

"Not a problem, Detective. We keep our footage for three months, then we send it to corporate, where it's also looked at by our other security analysts."

"Jake, can you just pull up what they asked for?" Mark questioned, seemingly aggravated by our presence.

Jake turned and began typing. Six of the twelve monitors lit up with new images, while the others continued surveillance of the store and entrance. After entering the time and date, he pressed a button that forwarded the video right up until fifteen minutes before Amber Seasons completed her purchase.

We could see in the video that our victim walked around with her selection in her hand, before pausing in front of a mirror to check herself out. She slung the gym bag over her shoulder, just as an athlete would, to where it was now out of sight. Amber then held a shirt up to her neckline. She posed briefly, modeling the shirt, before hanging it back on the wrong rack and walked off. I scanned the video looking for anyone that seemed out of place, while keeping my eyes glued to our victim.

"Can you fast forward to when she makes her purchase? I also want the parking lot, front entrance, both exits, and cashier cameras from that date and time pulled up, and run it at half speed please," I instructed Jake.

Eight forty-five p.m. read in the corner of each monitor. We all watched in silence. Amber Seasons' smile met with the cashier's eyes, eliciting a smile back. They exchanged unknown words momentarily. The cashier then handed her a receipt, which she signed and politely handed back. Her smile never wavered. No one at any of the other registers paid her any attention, or so it seemed.

"Can you zoom in on her, Jake?" Mitchell questioned.

The next image that came up of our victim was of her emerging outside of the exit door. She paused slowly, beckoning cars to continue passing while she seemed to ponder which way to go. Two cars passed by before she continued to the left side of the parking lot. She soon disappeared out of camera view.

"Where is she? Pull her back up," I demanded as I scanned each camera, even the ones I knew were only streaming present day footage. The room grew quiet momentarily. I felt I was speaking to myself. I knew something was awry when I noticed Mark lower his head. "Unfortunately, Detective Lane, this is out of view of our store's camera," Jake broke the silence.

"You have to be kidding me! So, you're telling me that those cameras that we saw in the parking lot are inoperable?" I scrutinized in disbelief, while studying the room for the dreaded response that I knew was coming.

"No...I mean, actually, yes. They weren't installed at that time. We just added those cameras last week with more lighting as added safety measures. We didn't have the budget for it. GameChangers is a family-owned store," he gave an excuse, when there was none needed.

"A little too late on the safety measures, huh, chief?" Mitchell commented.

"That was not an issue that I could foresee, nor did I have the power to make decisions about. Things happen, and I'm truly sorry that it happened at all, not just here." Although I didn't agree with what he said, I understood.

"I'll take the footage that you have, and that includes the footage from the days leading up to June 9th. Just maybe, whoever is involved in her abduction will be seen stalking or lingering around the premises. Also, could you provide me with a list of your employees that worked on that day. That should be all for now," I stated, giving him a short request list.

"I can have it on a drive for you in about twenty minutes," Jake replied, turning his focus to downloading the files and footage requested.

"You guys stated earlier that you were investigating a disappearance, but you aren't. You two are homicide detectives. This woman that you came to inquire about today is dead, isn't she?" Carlton, the

Sherlock Holmes of GameChangers Sporting Goods, made his discovery known. His facial expression let me know that he had already formulated an answer. Even so, I still obliged him in my response.

"Yes, her body was discovered a few days ago. This was her last known location."

"Son of a bitch, I knew I heard that name before. She's the daughter of those..." Carlton was cut off mid-sentence as Mark interjected.

"Yes, indeed, she frequently visited our store. I really hate this; she had a radiant personality with a bright future. I know this has to be a really sad time for her parents; they seemed to be good people."

Neither I, nor Mitchell, bothered to give a response regarding his statement. It wouldn't matter one way or another as we were out to catch a killer, not see who could win parent of the year.

"Mitchell and I are going to do a walk around the parking lot while you take care of the video footage. If you think of anything else that would be of use, please include it on the flash drive," I told Jake, thanking him as we exited the security room.

The massive parking lot left plenty of points of vulnerability. Analyzing it from an investigative point of view and not a customer, I could only imagine how dimly lit and vulnerable the parking lot was on the night of Amber's disappearance. For the next fifteen minutes, Mitchell and I canvassed the massive parking lot looking for any clues. Our killer, or killers, had plenty of vantage points that they could have stalked our victim from.

I glanced up at the various light poles scattered about, and I could see where some of the lights had been shot out. I also noticed that there were no roaming security guards riding around in a cart or police presence near the entrance as you would see at most major department stores.

"What time does this store close, Lane?"

"Ten p.m. Why?"

Mitchell walked over to where I stood. "Entertain me for a second.

This place closes at ten p.m., which would make it common knowledge that the parking lot would be pretty empty towards closing. That means Amber Seasons wouldn't have had to park far. If it were me, I would come out of a store, scan briefly for my car, then I'd make a beeline for it. I would look for any suspicious vehicles near mine, and for anyone roaming loosely in the parking lot."

" And… What's your point, Mitchell?"

"My point is this, we know for a fact that she didn't want to be taken, but even so, I don't think she was forced or involved in a violent struggle during her abduction. See, with this parking lot being practically empty at closing time, Amber Seasons was out in the open, which would be a very risky abduction, unless a ruse was involved."

"Are you saying she was tricked into a vehicle, while she had her car sitting several feet away?" I asked, still confused as to his point.

"It's a possibility, but what I'm saying is this. If Amber was the kind person that everyone is saying that she was, then it would make sense that she would extend a hand to help someone in need. Which would mean, there may be numerous possible suspects involved."

I stared at Mitchell briefly; his assertion came together well. "You actually make sense. Even if she were held at gunpoint, they would have had to be near her vehicle to commit the abduction. I highly doubt that they raced across the parking lot screaming 'freeze, don't move' at the top of their lungs."

Mitchell shook his head at my statement, as he did most times. He informed me that I was being "extra," a phrase he heard my daughter say several times concerning some of my conversations.

While Mitchell continued to speak words that I could no longer hear, time began to stand still. I looked on in silence as a white minivan pulled out of a parking space, almost dead center from the front entrance of the store. I began walking in the direction of the slow-moving vehicle, doing my best to get a look at the occupants. A mother and her two young boys stared back at me with curious expressions on their faces. I took a deep breath, then focused back on my new found discovery.

"Mitchell, I think we just caught our first break," I told him, pointing in the direction of the vehicle.

He snapped his neck around quickly to see what I was pointing at. "Well-well, I'll be damned, Lane," Mitchell responded, pointing in the same direction. "That looks like our victim's car."

"It most certainly does, Mitchell. You can call it in to be sure," I suggested to him, while donning a pair of nonlatex gloves and passing him a pair as well.

The doors of the vehicle were locked and each tire had been deflated. We did a quick walk around using our phones to record and take photos, while making notes. I made my stop at the driver's door then did a quick survey of my surroundings. I began putting myself into the victim's shoes, recreating the scene. In my search, I noticed one of the cameras facing our direction. If that camera would have been installed previous to the night Amber Seasons went missing, it would have been pointed directly at our victim's car. Plus, we could have seen the footage inside the security room. It was too bad those cameras were installed after her abduction.

It was obvious that she was a frequent customer here, who took her safety seriously, and expected GameChangers Sporting Goods to do the same. She may have thought that GameChangers would have some sort of security enforced in that area. Unfortunately for us, the same case couldn't be made for her abductors.

"Had those cameras been installed, we would have been able to see exactly what took place the evening of her disappearance," I announced my thoughts to Mitchell.

"You're right," he said.

"With her doors being locked, it is safe to say that she never got close enough to use her key fob to unlock her doors or set off the panic alarm, which would have drawn attention. I'm starting to believe that this was a well-thought-out abduction, and that no matter what our victim had done that night, it wouldn't have changed the outcome. Whoever did this was determined and beyond cunning," I said, realizing that I was giving our suspect or suspects a compliment.

"And if that's the case, Lane, this won't be their last either. I just got word that the CSU (Crime Scene Unit) is on the way, as well as the store manager," Mitchell added.

In a matter of minutes, flashing lights littered the parking lot, flashing silently at high-speed rates.

"Let's make sure this entire area is secure, Mitchell. I can already see the chaos about to begin."

CHAPTER FIFTEEN

MISSY

"Daphne, I don't know about you, but after I get some rest I want to see what the California nightlife has to offer. Do you want to hit the club scene later?"

"I don't know, you just landed not even a couple of hours ago. Are you sure you'll want to get out later?"

Daphne had always been skeptical about going anywhere with me and that was because I didn't put up with her BS and let her know it no matter what we were, while everyone else always turned a blind eye. Daphne was an only child until I was adopted, and her resentment for that was on full display while we were in our teens. We have since gotten over some of those issues, but I was here to support Gramma, and that would be in moderation.

"I slept the entire flight, until they announced we'd land shortly. If you don't want to go, just say so, I can hangout by myself." I could tell that she thought I was being smart, but I wasn't, and that was one of the things that I didn't like about her.

"Do you ever just answer a question? I don't know. If I'm up, then I'll go with you," she assured me.

"Catherine, why don't you accompany me over to my friend Georgia's house for some wine and cheese? You need your rest for tomorrow, and we won't be long at Georgia's," Gramma asked, extending an invite to an old ladies convention. The fact that she had just heard me ask Daphne not to call me Catherine, I should say no... I preferred Missy, and she knew that.

Daphne waited to see how I would respond, while Gramma walked away from both of us into the kitchen. She has gotten to the point where she rarely goes anywhere with me, so I think I'm going to hang out with her some."

I caught the questionable look Daphne gave her as she stood behind Gramma.

"Oh Gramma, I would've loved to hangout with you, but I just informed Daphne that I would go to the club with her."

Gramma looked at Daphne curiously. "You want to hang out with your sister?" she was befuddled.

"That's right. I invited her out for drinks." Daphne was assertive.

"Drinks, you say? Well, I hope that neither of you will be driving under the influence."

"No, of course not, Gramma. We'll catch a cab," I assured her.

"Well, okay then. I'm glad you guys will spend some quality time together," Gramma commented, before leaving the room.

"You're sure you don't wanna go out with Gramma, Catherine?" Daphne asked, putting emphasis on Gramma.

"Call me Catherine again Daphne, and I might just go hangout with her." I was serious.

"I wouldn't be surprised if you did. I want you to know that I'm not that precarious socialite you think I am. Matter of fact, I'm willing to bet you that your life in Atlanta is nothing like the adventure of mine," Daphne boasted.

I laughed uncontrollably at that notion.

"What's so funny?" I couldn't believe she asked me that question.

"You...You are, Daphne. What is your life like, huh? Is it full of mystery and action?"

"You're hilarious, I see. I'm going to get dressed, and we'll see who describes who best".

I met Daphne in the foyer a little over an hour after our conversation. I had to admit that she did look very different than I expected. Her style of dress was very provocative.

"You look nice, Daphne."

"You're not being funny are you, Missy?"

"I'm not," I assured her, thankful that she called me Missy and not Catherine.

We took several photos before our Uber arrived. It felt good to take some with her and not think about it as surveillance, although the photos we took would soon be deleted, by my hands. Our driver pulled into the parking lot, and I felt at home and alive as I took in the surrounding scenery. The club was humongous, and the line outside was long, as I expected.

"Daphne, we are not waiting in this line," I told her as I made my way to one of the security guards that seemed to be willing to make an extra buck. "Hey, this line is way too long for me to be holding my bladder, what would it take for my sister and I to get in and forgo this long line?"

The security guard ogled me up and down. "You say it's just two of ya'll?"

"Yes, my sister is right over there." I waved back towards Daphne. "I'm about to piss on myself. How much will it cost? Give me a number."

"Eighty dollars for the both of you," he recited what was probably his standard rate. I handed him the money and waited for Daphne to come over to us. The security guard escorted us to where we were searched and let in. The music was blaring and the crowd was a nice sized one, soon to get larger with the line waiting outside.

It seemed as if everyone had a drink in their hand but us. "Daphne, let's go over to the bar and order a couple of drinks." She agreed and followed me to the bar.

We ordered our drinks, then began commenting on guys that we saw. "Look at his hair, I think it may be time to just cut it all off," Daphne said to me, appearing to be having a good time.

I was finishing my drink when I was approached by a guy. I smelled him before he spoke, which made me give him my attention once he started talking. He was extremely handsome with an athletic build, and his cologne was intoxicating, so I decided to see what he had to say.

"Hi, my name is Brent. You two ladies are looking lovely. You're not from around here, are you?" he whispered in my ear.

"Why does it matter, Brent?" He shrugged his shoulders and was about to continue speaking until I cut him off.

"Look, dude, I'm sure you get your way by that line maybe 2 out of 10 times, which is a terrible percentage, but it shows you that your approach doesn't work. I'm going to give you a little advice, Brent. See, most men would have started off the conversation with an introduction, followed by an offer to refill our glasses. Here I am holding an empty glass that I'm about to replace on my own dime, so if you don't have any other questions, I'll be seeing you around," I informed him, then turned my back to him.

Brent apparently hadn't heard a word that I had said, as he was still standing next to me sipping his drink. Daphne glanced in his direction but continued to dance, not caring about what we were discussing.

"So, I take it that you didn't hear anything that I just said." I wanted to know why he was still next to me.

Brent laughed, then moved a little closer to me to where I could now see his features better. I found that he had a nice smile.

"Hey, I apologize for my approach. I'm going to start over. Hi, my name is Brent, and yours?"

"I'm Missy," I entertained him

"Nice to meet you, Missy. I see that your drink is low, would you like a refill for yourself and your friend, if she would like one, while we get to know each other?"

"That was much better. It's all about respect. I wasn't trying to be an ass. We will take you up on your offer, Brent. I'm drinking Patron, and my sister, who is not my friend, is drinking Grey Goose," I corrected him.

We found Brent to be a cool guy. He had a good conversation with us, and a good sense of humor to accompany it. We spent most of the night at the bar dancing in place and drinking. I could tell that Daphne was starting to get bored by the way she kept looking around, so I wasn't in the least surprised when she whispered into my ear. "It's getting late Sis, how long do you plan on hanging out?"

"I don't have a certain time, or a curfew, Daphne. Plus, I'm not quite ready to go." The look on her face let me know that wasn't what she wanted to hear.

"We have a lot to do tomorrow, and you are aware of this. I'm not saying we have to leave now, I just don't want to be out all night."

"I can understand that. Let me see what Brent is about to get into, and we'll go from there," I told her, as I didn't want the night to end just yet. There was no way to know when would be the next time I could enjoy myself out in public with the life I truly lived, so I was going to take full advantage of this night.

I hadn't been with a man in a long time, and Brent looked like the perfect candidate. He must have read the look on my face, so I sipped my drink seductively while looking at him.

"Everything alright?" he questioned, leaning in close, ensuring I got another whiff of his cologne.

"Everything is fine. What do you have planned after you leave here?" I asked him.

"Home to bed, most likely, why? What are your plans after leaving here?"

"My plans after leaving here include you, if you're down for some fun."

"I'm having fun now," he answered, obviously oblivious to exactly what I was proposing.

I grabbed him by the arm, then pulled him slightly away from where Daphne couldn't hear us. "This place has run its course. My sister and I would like to go back to your place and explore our options a little further in an intimate setting, if you know what I mean." Brent gave an acknowledging nod. I knew he would be thrilled at the idea of having two women back to his place, willing and ready.

Now all I had to do was convince Daphne to go along. I approached her and gave her my idea of a good night; I added the fact that we definitely wouldn't be touching each other, just enjoying Brent.

Even though we're only sisters by adoption, the thought of touching her still wasn't appealing in my eyes.

Daphne was appalled by the mere suggestion. "Are you fucking kidding me?"

"Calm down, it's just a question that you can say yes or no to. I thought you lived adventurously, or is the word vicariously I'm looking for, Sis?" I posed, being facetious.

"The word that you're looking for is fool, and you're on if you think I would agree to something like this. I thought this night would be different from any other night that we've tried to do the sisterly thing, but as usual, you find a way to ruin it." Daphne took a large gulp of her drink, then walked away from me without saying a word. I didn't have time for her dramatics.

"Hey Brent, nevermind her; you wouldn't have liked her anyway. She's a vibe killer, and can be a real stiff, if you know what I mean. I'm not giving up on a trio, how about you stay right here, and give me a few minutes to find her replacement."

"Are you sure you don't need my help?" Brent asked me, his confidence was attractive.

"I'm positive, this isn't my first rodeo. You relax, have another drink, and I'll make sure that it'll be two women going home with you, instead of one." Brent pulled me in by my waist. I liked his aggressiveness.

"Don't take too long, as you stated, this isn't my first rodeo, either." His point was well taken. It was good to know I wouldn't have to be a coach, once we made it back to his place.

"I'll be back before you can finish your drink". I surveyed the club, looking for things that had to be aligned for me to approach one of these women. They had to be alone, inebriated, and pretty. The best place to find a person that easily fit that description was usually at the ladies room. Those women constantly check their make-up, drink water while they consume alcohol, so they're in the restroom often.

I spotted an attractive woman standing near the hallway leading to the restroom. I gathered that either she was waiting on someone, or just making a call in one of the only spots she could hear. I waited until she completed her call to see what she would do.

The woman placed her phone inside her purse, then shook her head as if frustrated by the call. "Hey, are you in line, or waiting on someone?" I questioned, acting as if I needed to check my makeup. I could tell that whoever she had called had disappointed her. "Are you okay?" I feigned concern.

"I'm okay, why do you ask? Is it that obvious?"

"I wouldn't say that because you seem like you're good at hiding your emotions, but you don't look like you're having fun."

"You're absolutely right. My friend was supposed to meet me here, then ended up canceling once I made it inside. I paid forty dollars to park damnit and forty to get in, and I was going to try to have a few drinks and see how the night turned out. Even though it's a nice crowd, I'm not feeling it." The opportunity has presented itself, and I wasn't about to miss it.

"My name is Missy, what's yours?"

"I'm Nadia." She placed her cup in the hand she clutched her purse under, then extended her hand for me to shake. I reciprocated.

"Nadia, that's a beautiful name. I was just telling my friend that I was bored and would like to leave shortly."

"Are you guys going to another club?" She seemed interested.

"I doubt it. We will probably head over to his place, and hangout there. If you don't have anything going on after you leave here, maybe you can drop by. I'm not in California much, which is why I plan on making the most of the nights that I am here." I reached out and gently stroked her arm. She didn't recoil, as the look on her face let me know that she knew that I was flirting.

"I'm not really into women," she stated, but never stopped my hand from rubbing.

"I'm not into women that much either, but I am into…" I pointed in the direction of Brent, who, as if on cue, flashed that brilliant smile of his. "I have someone I want you to meet. Is that okay?" The woman nodded, then took a nervous sip of her drink. Brent walked casually, dodging club goers in the process, while not spilling a drop of his drink. I sure hoped like hell that he would just follow my lead once he made it over.

"Hey, Brent," I greeted, before grabbing him by the chin, then kissed him on his lips. Brent went with the flow and even further when he placed one hand on my waist, and the other on my ass. He forced his tongue inside of my mouth, and I broke the embrace, then returned my attention to Nadia.

"Whew…so are you up for some fun tonight?" I offered, fanning myself as if Brent's kiss had an effect on me, before I reached to grab Nadia's hand.

"What type of fun are you talking about?" she questioned as she eyed Brent.

"I'm sure that you've heard the expression, 'I can show you, better than I can tell you'? Well, that is the case here. All you have to do is follow my lead…that goes for you too Brent. It's your call, didn't you say that you were bored?" I reiterated her words.

Nadia shrugged her shoulders, and chuckled while replying. "What the heck…I'm up for some fun."

"Awesome, so what are we waiting on?" Brent questioned, then grabbed me by the hand, which I in turn grabbed Nadia's hand, then he led us off the club dance floor into a secluded corner opposite the restroom area. He suddenly stopped. I gave him a questioning look.

"Is everything alright?" I asked.

Brent reached behind me, then pulled Nadia up into his arms. She looked at him as if he was half crazy.

"I wanted you to know that we are going to my place, and I'm not the type of person to where I live without I, or them, knowing fully what we are going there for. I want to be sure that you are on the same page as us," Brent told her. At this point, I was also looking at her for an answer.

Nadia, placed her hand into the middle of Brent's chest, then backed him into the wall. She leaned in close to him as if she was about to kiss him, then moved her mouth around to his ear. I wasn't sure what she had told him, but the look on his face let me know that it was exactly what he wanted to hear.

Nadia backed away then grabbed me by the hand. "Now that we got that settled, can we leave?" I was turned on.

"No, there's one more thing," Brent stated before reaching into his pocket and retrieving a small tube with about five pills in it. "Here, take these, and by the time we get back to my place they will be in full effect." He was ecstatic as he envisioned how things would play out.

I used drugs to sedate people all the time, leaving the rendered helpless. It wasn't a drug that I didn't know about and the effects that it caused. I wasn't against taking recreational drugs, but with my life-style, it wasn't conducive. However, I wasn't living in that world at this moment.

"Are these clean?" I questioned. He handed me one to inspect. They were authentic. Nadia had already taken hers before I could let her know that they were legit. People passed away from synthetic drugs daily due to how easily they can be replicated.

"Of course, they are," he assured us, before placing a pill on his tongue. He took the last sip of his cup and sat it down.

"Where are we going? To your place that you hopefully live alone at?" I wanted to know, my own thoughts of being deceitful had crept in.

"Yeah, sure. Of course, I have a nice oceanfront condo on the beach, with a captivating view of the ocean, even at night," he boasted.

"Sounds good, let's get out of here," I declared, that was until I spotted Daphne standing alone looking around.

"Hey Brent, I need to go say something to my sister. I'll meet you guys out front." They agreed, and I made my way over to Daphne. I gave a half truth.

"Hey, I didn't think you were still here," I told her.

"I'm about to leave, I was just tracking my Uber. Are you leaving with me?" she questioned, as she continued to look at her phone and finish her drink.

"No, I'm not going with you. I'm leaving with Brent. We're going to hangout at his place."

"Are you sure that's a wise decision? You don't know him." She was concerned. But she had no idea that I was fully trained in every martial arts and hand to hand combat. I trained with a former marine three times a week, Mister, who was twice Brent's size.

"I'll be ok. Brent is not a threat to my safety, plus we have another woman with us. I will see you in the morning. Please let me know that you made it home safely," I told her, showing my concern for her as well.

"I will." Daphne caught me off guard when she reached out and gave me a hug. I held her a little longer than expected.

"I'll see you in the morning, and don't let Gramma know that we didn't come home together either," I warned her, knowing that it wouldn't go well if Gramma found out.

Daphne nodded, then I walked away to enjoy what was sure to be an eventful night.

CHAPTER SIXTEEN
DETECTIVE LANE

"Based on the nature of the crimes and the ages of our victims, it would be safe to say that a female might have a hand in these abductions. Detective Lane, if you would, could you make your way up here so that you can elaborate more?" Lieutenant Johnson beckoned with a flick of his wrist.

He and I had rarely spoken to each other, so I was taken aback by his invitation. I crept slowly up to where he stood.

"Being that you are lead detective, there may be something you can share that would corroborate what our profilers already came up with, if you don't mind."

I was hesitant, because honestly, my profile was a contrast to what our profiler just put together. I didn't want to give my opinion and it was completely wrong, which in turn would jeopardize our chances of catching our killers. There were definitely two suspects that I was sure of, but aside from that assessment, I would be spitting in the wind and that's not how I operate.

"Well, Lane, sometime today would be great," Lieutenant Johnson urged me on, drawing a few chuckles from both male and female police officers.

I smiled nervously before speaking. "I believe our killers are male and female, but I don't think they are a young duo. I believe our killers are between the ages of 34 and 40 with no employment, but they have a good income allowing them to move inconspicuously. They are very meticulous for sure, leaving behind no clues, and ensuring that the bodies are clean and positioned strategically. As we noticed in the slide earlier, both of our victims were athletic, which leads me to believe that the killers are athletic as well. To have the gall to approach these women that have been doing strength training for years, one of which was also a blackbelt. I believe that our victims' social status is a major factor in them being chosen, gender as well, so far."

I asked the woman working the projector to place a slide on before continuing on. "As you look at the screen, you can see that some sort of marking was drawn on her face. It may represent something symbolic, or it might be a calling card, which out of the two, I'm not sure of as of yet. I don't believe these markings are meant to look sadistic."

"It looks like a teardrop," someone yelled out

"It does a little." I had to agree because it was also my guess when I first saw it. "We see these tattoo markings under the eyes of gang members all the time. They are symbolic markings for killing an enemy."

"So if that's the look they're aiming for, they're doing a damn good job with that," someone else blurted out.

"That's enough, let's be quiet so she can finish up," Lieutenant Johnson ordered.

"I was saying earlier, with the crime scenes that we have processed, none have turned up any evidence or witnesses that actually saw something. I actually don't have much to say, Lieutenant, so if no one has a question, I'll return to my seat." I began making my way away from the podium when a question was posed.

"Detective Lane, you mentioned earlier that you believe this couple to be financially stable, enough to move about freely and safely, right?"

"What I said was, that the suspect or suspects according to my profile, have a good source of income," I corrected him.

"Oh, okay, good. Because I couldn't imagine having some sick, rich fucks out here killing kids for symbolic reasons."

"Honestly, it wouldn't be the first time it has happened, but I don't think they are a couple at all. I do think that they work like a well organized duo team with a common goal in mind. Something binds them together that allows them to trust the other's decision making to not have made a mistake up to this far point."

"I don't follow you with that statement," Lieutenant Johnson spoke up.

This was exactly why I didn't want to come to the podium. Everything that I said now was all speculation. The more that I said, could mean the more I would later have to take back or explain later, but as the Lieutenant looked on for an answer, I gave him my thoughts.

"In this world we always hear people referred to as 'Alpha male or Alpha female', most people don't identify and realize that there are Alpha plus people out there, that no matter what environment that they happen to be in, they are the leader. In this case, we have two true alpha pluses paired together, and one has willingly given up their power for the greater cause, whatever that might be. In their rationale, they believe that they are doing some sort of justice." I had speculated enough.

"There is nothing rational about anything they're doing," Lieutenant Johnson stated the obvious.

"You're right, but in their mind, it is. And to catch them, we have to figure out what exactly that entails. We have to try to see things through their eyes."

The room went eerily silent. Lieutenant Johnson placed a hand on my shoulder. "Thank you for providing your opinion as to giving us an idea of who or what we are possibly dealing with."

"You're welcome, Lieutenant. This will require all hands to be on deck."

"Speaking of all hands on deck, the higher ups have already instructed me to give you the department's full resources from every unit in this room."

I didn't know what to say. I knew that this case was getting attention that it normally didn't, and I was starting to feel something was amiss. I knew that I was right when he proceeded on with a direct offer to me in front of the entire room.

"Detectives Lane and Mitchell, you are to report directly to me. Your Sergeant has already been informed. All information will be distributed on a need to know basis."

I felt blindsided, and for him to exclude Sarge was beyond me. He and I didn't have a relationship, and as a lieutenant, what could he do with the information I gave him but share it himself? I wanted to address what I saw developing, but I knew this was not the right platform to do so. Mitchell was standing at the back of the room, and I watched him raise his coffee cup in a mock toast after that announcement.

At that moment, I knew that I'd been made his scapegoat. Hence, if anything went wrong, Mitchell and I would take the fall. I made eye contact with Mitchell. He nodded in my direction with an approving smile. We already knew how to play this game, if that's how they wanted to play.

"From now until the day we apprehend our suspects, we'll have a debriefing at least once daily, starting at 0845," I stated, while looking Lieutenant Johnson in his eyes. "If there are no further questions or comments, I'd like to be excused, as I have a case to solve." I walked away without waiting on a response.

CHAPTER SEVENTEEN

MISSY

Nadia and I lay on the bed naked under the cool of the ceiling fan and the breeze coming in from the beach. Brent stood near his entertainment system searching for a good playlist he had informed us. His entertainment system came to life, and music reminiscent of the club began resonating through the surround sound speakers that were attached to the bed. I could tell that Brent didn't have any money issues as his room was immaculate for a man that lived alone.

"Would you ladies like a refill?" Brent pulled the champagne that we had been drinking out of the ice bucket and refilled our glasses. I tracked his movements as he sat the bottle down on his bookshelf. I watched him adjust a book that didn't need adjusting in my eyes before he slowly made his way over to the bed.

Brent grabbed a handful of Nadia's hair, then engaged in a sensual kiss with her that was full of passion. One would have thought that they were lovers. I was turned on, but I remained still and continued to sip on my glass as he removed hers from her hand and laid her on her back. At this point, I didn't need an invitation as I watched him slide his tongue down her body to her vagina. Nadia grabbed me by the head forcefully and pulled me in to her for a kiss. It felt natural, and I relaxed and rubbed her breast softly.

Brent reached out and slung my legs open, breaking Nadia and I's kiss. He roughly pulled me to him, then parted my legs. He dove into me with his tongue as if I were a pool. My legs had a mind of their own as they floated in the air, giving him full access. I was moaning, and it didn't help that Nadia was now rubbing my breast while licking them. I was on the verge of my first organic orgasm in years. "Oh my fucking…" I couldn't even finish the sentence. I couldn't even catch my breath before Brent was trying to mount me.

"Do you have protection?" I managed to say. He looked aggravated. He bounced off the bed and entered the bathroom. He returned with a box of magnums. He opened the box and before he could put it on, Nadia was on him.

She sat at the end of the bed while he stroked in and out of her mouth. I slid over to them, and began to place soft kisses onto his stomach until I was rewarded with his shaft in my mouth. I could see why Brent walked around with the confidence that he had shown when we first met. He hadn't disappointed in any area as of yet. He pumped in on out of my lips while he used his fingers to keep Nadia occupied. We were moving in harmony.

I wanted to feel every inch of him, so I leaned my head back and slid back to the middle of the bed. Brent placed the condom on and climbed on top of me. He lifted my left leg to where it was near his shoulder and used his right hand to guide himself inside of me. I let out a low gasp, he felt so good. I placed my hands on his waist, and we each worked up to a rhythm that satisfied us both.

Nadia had now come to my side and was back placing kisses all over my body, sending waves of electricity, enhanced from the drugs and alcohol, to another level. I began to shutter as I was about to reach my climax. Nadia held my hand like a comforting nurse during a surgery as my body jerked and shook for what seemed like a few minutes. Brent pulled out of me, then switched condoms and proceeded to pound Nadia from the back.

I caught my breath, and we continued to change positions and enjoy each other for what seemed like hours before Brent announced that he had to use the bathroom...

"I have to go to the bathroom," he told us. Brent returned from the bathroom with three damp rags. He gave Nadia and I one apiece, then he laid on his back and began cleaning himself off.

"Are we done?" Nadia caught us off guard.

"I'm not, just taking a breather, you ladies are a handful."

I waited until he finished wiping himself, before I grabbed his soft penis, and began making it hard with my mouth. Brent removed his hands from behind his head, and placed one on mine, guiding my head up on down. I got him as hard as I could before coming up.

"I want you to fuck her, and fuck her hard," I told him, sounding as seductive as I could.

Brent looked at me as if I was joking. "Are you--are you for real?"

"Yes, I want to watch you fuck her roughly." Nadia, not one to need instruction, turned her ass toward Brent, then spread her cheeks, giving him full access to his target. Brent looked at me, then placed her in the middle of the bed and adjusted her to where she was now facing the book shelf.

Brent licked his fingers, but this time he didn't place a condom on. He rubbed himself, coating his penis, before entering Nadia forcefully. Her gasp wasn't one of pleasure, which turned me on even more. I began inserting my fingers in and out of my vagina while landing back shot after back shot, causing Nadia to cry out in pain and pleasure. He was pumping in and out of her with a furious pace, slapping her on her ass.

"Pull her hair," I ordered. Brent obliged. Sweat was popping off him, and for a second, I thought he was going to pass out. I could tell he was about to reach a climax, when he took his hand of her hair and placed it on her waist. His strokes became slower.

"Don't come in me," Nadia yelled out as she could tell he was about to release his load soon.

Brent snatched out of Nadia just in time, and began spewing cum all over her back and ass. Nadia fell forward laying on her stomach as if she needed a chalk outline around her. He had sure done what I'd asked, but it was nothing like watching Mister do his thing.

I heard the doorbell and a loud knock at the door, which I had already known who would be coming. "Brent, I thought you lived alone. It's like 4 a.m., who could this be?" I questioned feigning concern.

"Hell, I don't know, maybe it's a neighbor." He stood up and grabbed a pair of boxers before going to the door. Nadia and I followed him to see who it was. I wasn't shocked as I saw Daphne standing there. I already sent her my location, and I gave her specific instructions. I saw that she had my bag that I asked her to bring, which brought me chills.

"Well, well, you didn't tell me that you invited your sister. I thought you said she was a stiff?" He quoted my words, and I watched the facial expression on Daphne's face.

"Well, she can't speak for me, and I'm not here for that. I came to pick my sister up," Daphne responded.

"I had her come by to get me. I'm sure that you're not taking me home, plus Nadia might not be ready to leave, and she drove herself. I hope that isn't a problem." I didn't want his radar up.

"No, it's fine, but..." He let Daphne in, then placed his hands around her waist. "You might as well have fun while you're here." I was disgusted as he grabbed her ass. Daphne managed to play it cool.

"I live in California, we'll get together another time…maybe when my sister isn't involved." I knew that she was bullshitting. Brent removed his hands, then moved aside.

"If that's the case, then welcome to my humble abode, glad you could join us…well at least stop by."

"Do you mind if I use the bathroom? It was a long ride. The alcohol from earlier is still running through me." Daphne was doing so well that one would think she knew my plans.

"Sure, I guess you can use the one in the bedroom." he said, granting her permission.

We followed Brent back into the bedroom. I began to gather all of my things, then got dressed. Nadia chose to lay back down, and I didn't bother to stop her.

"I'm going to get some rest, the sun will be up in a few hours, if that's okay with you, Brent," she proclaimed.

"Sure, are you sure you're going to sleep? I mean, it's about to just be the two of us," he retorted then sat down next to her with his back to me.

He was right. It was just about to be only them. Daphne came out of the bathroom, and Brent never looked up, because if he did, he might have seen the long barber style razor blade that she handed me.

"Oh fuck!" Daphne screamed before I could reach around and slit Brent's entire throat. I managed to cut him enough that he had to place both hands on his neck. He rolled onto the floor, then backed himself against the wall.

His eyes bulged with fear as I approached him with all intent to finish what I started. Blood was coming out his mouth, letting me know that he was trying to speak. Nadia had her legs glued to her chest and was screaming out of her mind.

"Shut her up!" I told Daphne, who was just looking at me for direction. "It doesn't matter, Daphne, just shut her up!" I demanded.

I was surprised when Daphne pulled out a gun, and shot the woman in the chest. Nadia's eyes met mine as she fell backwards against the headboard. Daphne dropped the gun, then placed her hands on top of her head in frustration.

"What the fuck Missy…what in the entire fuck!?"

I had no time to answer her, as I saw Brent trying to get up. I rushed over and kicked him in his chest, causing his hands to fly away from his neck. I was on him swinging my blade wildly, he used his arms as a defense like that was going to stop me. I hit several arteries to the point his arms just lay at his side. He was coated with sweat and blood, but still alive. I lifted his chin.

"Do you know why this happened you fucking creep?" I walked over to the bookshelf, then I adjusted the same book that he had. What was there was a small remote. They didn't have to ask what I was doing as the words recording were still blinking in red.

"You see this Daphne? This is what he was doing. He was secretly recording us, and there is no telling how many other women he has done this to," I said before I walked back over to Brent and pulled him by his hair. "You perverted sonofabitch! I didn't want to have to do this to you, but I can't be a part of your fucking collection, when I have my own," I told him before slitting his throat completely. The warm blood splashing on me was exhilarating.

Daphne was now screaming as she witnessed me enjoying the bloodbath that I just caused. I stood up, and wiped my face with my blood soaked shirt. "He deserved what he got, Sis, and she couldn't walk out of here after what I had planned to do to him."

"Where-where- did you learn to be like that? I'm not okay with this." I knew that I had to let Daphne see exactly who I was, or she wouldn't leave this condo as well.

"Daphne there is a lot that you don't know about me, but as I stated, this sick fuck got everything that he deserved; Nadia was just a part of the process and not your fault. I need you to know that what happened here today, doesn't leave here." I placed my hand on her shoulder, while still clutching the blade in the other. Daphne's gun lay on the floor below us, so I picked it up and handed it to her. "Do you understand what I just told you?" I shook her slightly

"Yes…yes, I understand, Missy. I don't want to spend the rest of my life in jail, so you don't have to worry about me saying anything."

"Good. Get Nadia's keys, and I'll drive her car away from here and dispose of it. Don't worry about me getting home, I'll be there before the sun comes up. I'm about to burn this place down to the ground," I told her. Daphne and I worked as a team ensuring that every inch of the bedroom was covered with accelerants. I let her leave, ensuring that she left with her lights off, then I set the condo ablaze. I jumped into Nadia's car, already knowing where to take it for disposal. I turned her radio up, feeling so alive; there was nothing like an unplanned kill to get the blood flowing.

CHAPTER EIGHTEEN

DETECTIVE LANE

"Lane, they have an ID on a second victim," Mitchell stated nonchalantly, sitting the file on my desk. I picked up the file and read it silently, while he said it aloud, standing over me.

"Carla Mango, 22 years of age, freshman at Georgia Tech. Do you notice the similarities?" Mitchell questioned.

"Give me a second." I continued to read on. Mitchell walked around to his desk. "Fuck…She's the daughter of some prominent people as well. This could get ugly quick, Mitchell"

"You're telling me! Can you imagine the hysteria once the media finds out they're targeting female athletes? And not to mention those of affluent families."

"Wait a minute, Mitchell. Who's to say that both being athletes aren't just a coincidence, we can't assume anything. The fact is that they are young, wealthy, Caucasian women, are things that aren't assumptions. We need to send a request through to GBI (Georgia Bureau of Investigation) to see if they get a hit of any case similar to what we are seeing.

"We can't just sit on this, Lane and have another student get abducted."

"What do you suggest then, Mitchell? Are you insinuating that we call every college campus head of security in the state of Georgia, and have then shut down their sports program?" Mitchell looked disrespected. "Look, I understand what you're suggesting, Mitchell, and I apologize for that outburst, but let's not forget that I have a daughter, who is also an athlete in college."

"Who is an athlete in college? June?"

"That's another story, but soon to be, so she says. This is my call Mitchell, at least until we hear back from GBI. The only people that should be conscious of anything are the men and women that are a part of our task force, for now."

Mitchell threw up his arms in defeat. "If you say so, Lane. I can use a strong coffee, I'll be back." I knew exactly where Mitchell was headed after making that statement. Drinking while on duty is not allowed, but that's not to say it doesn't happen. Officers are not running around in a drunken stupor, but a shot in a cup of coffee has been the go-to drink for men and women in law enforcement forever. The reason I didn't want that for Mitchell was because his drinking almost cost him his career while he went through his father passing away.

"Hey…you good?"

"I'm good, why do you ask? Oh, okay. No, I'm not going down that road again, Lane, so you don't have to worry about me in that way."

"Cool, just making sure. Go ahead, and I'll send this information out." Mitchell walked towards me, gave me a thumbs up then walked away.

I sat there lost in thought, as I stared at the name on the top of the folder. The whole idea of teenage college girls being abducted was nothing new. They were easily accessible, not ones that pay attention to their surroundings as they focus on so many other things. I thought about June, and of the things that could be running through her mind as she went from class to class.

I also thought about how college students plaster so much of their personal information on the internet, such a location, and they do it consistently to the point a person could know the exact day and time to abduct someone. I was almost sure that whoever these women abductors may be, they most likely never had prior contact, maybe not in person with either of them, but that was usually not the case.

With that thought, I decided to reach out to an old friend, as the idea of our suspects not being a local duo filled my thoughts. It didn't hurt to have the GBI search similarities in Georgia, while my contact in the FBI searched globally. It only be a matter of time before the FBI was involved anyway, if this continued in the direction I was thinking it would.

"Special Agent Rush, how may I help you?," his baritone voice boomed through the receiver. I hesitated briefly, realizing the door that I was opening just by initiating contact. Not only was I foregoing protocol by involving a federal agent in a case my supervisors hadn't permitted me to do, but I was also initiating contact with a past lover.

"Hello," I replied softly

"Tracy? Tracy? Is that you?" He sounded happy to hear my voice.

"It's me."

"Hold for a second." I listened as he told whoever was in his office to leave. "Hey, how are you, what's going on?"

"I'm fine, Bryon, I hope that you have been to, as well as your wife." There was a brief silence before he responded. I heard his familiar uncomfortable chuckle. "It's funny you should mention her, Tracy."

"Didn't seem like a funny question to me, Bryon," I replied, confused.

"I apologize. You don't know, do you? How would you?"

"Know what?"

"Well, Felicia and I have been divorced for over two years now. Last I heard, she was dating a councilman from New Jersey, not that I care or anything."

I can't say that I was surprised, or that I felt any sympathy for him after how our relationship ended in deceit. "I'm sorry to hear that," I managed to still get out.

"No need to be sorry. It was inevitable. Our relationship was never the same after we left Atlanta."

At that moment, I began to regret making this phone call even more. Bryon and I had a brief three-month affair while his wife, a lobbyist, was out on the campaign trail. In the beginning, I didn't know that he was married, but after spending as much as we were able to together, I didn't care anymore. Our rendezvous were very discreet, and I never disrespected his wife by violating the side woman code. Bryon on the other hand couldn't stick to his own rules, which led to us almost getting caught. Instead of his wife trying to see who the other woman was, she took a job in Washington, and Byron, like the dutiful husband he was, followed.

This would be only the second time that he and I have spoken since. There was no need to drag this conversation out any more than I already had. "Bryon, I need your help."

The inflection in his voice changed immediately. "Sure. Anything, Tracy, just name it." I scanned the room to see if anyone was in earshot before I spoke.

"I have a case that…" he cut me off.

"Are you calling me from your cell phone?"

"Yes, why?"

"Hang up and go downstairs to Records, and see Thomas Ritten-wire. Tell him I sent you, and he'll handle the rest," he rambled off.

"What? Why can't I…"

"Tracy, just do it."

"Alright, alright."

"Hey… it's so nice to hear your voice. I've never stopped thinking about you," he told me, and the line went silent.

"Hello?" I called out. Now wasn't the time to get into the type of conversation that was needed between us. Whether he knew it or not, I also never stopped thinking about him, but not in the way that he might have wanted me to. Bryon will always hold a special place in my heart, but it is one that he would never get close to again. I was just about to stand up when Mitchell reappeared.

"Gotcha some chamomile tea, as a peace offering." He held out the cup, and I looked at it questionably. "Don't worry, neither mine nor yours has anything other than what it should have in it." I took the cup and smiled.

"To peace." We toasted.

"Where are you headed?"

"I'm going to talk to Thomas in Records. I'll be back in a few."

"Did you send the information to G.B.I yet?" he questioned.

"Nope, you can handle it while I'm gone." I watched as he shook his head in disappointment while I headed to the elevator.

CHAPTER NINETEEN

DETECTIVE LANE

It was nine-fifteen a.m., and we'd been sitting in the morgue lobby waiting for the Chief M.E., and my friend, Anessa Leggett, to conclude her morning meeting. Her meetings were usually very detail oriented as they involved the discussion of the deaths that occurred from the time she left the building up into now. There was always a body to be processed every morning, whether from natural causes or other means. Some didn't have a family, friend, or significant other to claim them; instead, they stayed in state custody. I watched as the doors to the conference room opened up, and a crew with lab coats filed out, but Dr. Leggett wasn't one of them. I did see the Assistant Chief M..E, Dr. Stern, then headed in his direction, with Mitchell close behind.

Dr. Stern noticed us approaching and held up his finger as he was in a conversation. He ended his conversation prematurely as the person continued to try to say something, but he had already focused his attention on us.

"Good morning Dr. Stern, do you happen to know where Dr. Leggett is? She was supposed to meet us here to discuss the case after her morning meeting."

"Dr. Leggett won't be in today. She had a family emergency right before she was headed to the office," he told us.

"Is everything okay, did she say what happened?" I asked, because he was aware of our relationship.

"You know your friend, she's very private, but I don't think it was anything too serious. She was pretty calm when she gave instructions to me." I was happy to hear that.

"Good to hear. Dr. Stern, do you know if she left the file that she planned to go over with us?" I hoped like heck that she did.

"As a matter of fact, she did mention something about you guys coming by, but not about a file. If you follow me, I'll go into her office and grab it, then we can go into my office. Dr. Stern came out of her office with a file that was larger than most files we saw.

"Is that it?" I asked, rhetorically.

"Yes, follow me." He led us into his office, offered us seats, then took up residence behind his cluttered desk. He had the look of a man that was overworked, underpaid, and stressed out. "All I have is sparkling water, if you guys would like something to drink."

"No, thank you," I replied knowing that sparkling water wasn't Mitchell's drink of choice either.

Dr. Stern pulled off his wire-rimmed glasses off his thin and chiseled face, then placed them on his desk on top of some anonymous file. "How can I help you detectives with this file? Dr. Leggett didn't provide me with any instructions," he asked as if the job of entertaining requests of detectives grew tiresome.

"Dr. Stern, we first need to know if the body of Amber Seasons is still here, more so than what's in the file, that will be coming with us anyway," Mitchell stated.

"I'm not sure, I didn't have anyone on the manifest out to the funeral home this morning, so I assume that whomever that you're looking for should be here," he replied, also implying he had no clue who Amber Seasons was, which seemed odd.

In Dr. Stern's profession, I knew that it was best for his own mental health that he rarely thought about his patients after he or his staff were done with them. What I found to be odd, was that he didn't acknowledge the victim by name when it was well known that he knew her parents. "When was she here?" he followed up.

"About a week and a half ago," I told him, crossing my fingers subconsciously. "We desperately need one more look at her body before it is handed back to the family." I stressed the importance.

"I seriously doubt it. I'm sure by now that the family has made arrangements with the funeral home to come pick up the body. Just a second, though, I'll check. What did you say the name was?" He readied himself to type the name in on his computer

"Amber Seasons." His head perked up as he retrieved his glasses from the desk, then wrapped them around his ears.

"Are you fucking kidding me?" I had never heard Dr. Stern cuss in all the years I'd known him. "Amber Seasons? Howard's daughter? My goodness no." He removed his glasses again, letting them fall freely from his hands.

"Dr. Stern, are you okay?" Mitchell inquired "Do you need a drink? You look flushed."

"Please, grab me a bottle of water out of the mini fridge" Beads of sweat were dripping off of his forehead. He removed his lab coat while sitting, doing his best to cool himself off.

"Here you go." Mitchell handed him the bottle after removing the top.

"Thank you," he said before downing some of the beverage. "This is sad…I hate that a good friend and colleague of mine has to experience such a horrific tragedy. I just came back from vacation, so you have to excuse me, this is all new to me." He took a deep breath, then retrieved his glasses and placed them securely on his nose before picking up the phone and dialing a number.

Mitchell and I looked at each other, both hoping that, for some reason, her body would still be there. I did my best to read his facial expressions as he nodded his head up and down followed by the occasional yes. Dr. Stern hung up the phone, then intertwined his fingers and placed them on his desk.

"Well, is she here, Doc?"

"She's in the back. She's not fully put back together because of the removal of the fetus. A DNA sample on the fetus was requested."

"By whom?" I question vehemently. "The parents?" I already knew the answer to that question.

"I'm sorry, but you know I can't disclose that. I can, however, take you to the body," he told me before standing and leading us out the door.

Dr. Stern led us to a room that was converted from a storage room due to the frequent caseload. He walked around the covered up, but deceased bodies, as if they were pieces of furniture and nothing more. He quickly scanned the toe tags, and within minutes, he was signaling us to come over.

Amber's corpse was covered in a clean white linen sheet that gave her a real ghostly appeal. What I knew to be her fetus sat on a small table in a large beaker labeled 'John Doe Jr.', floating in a solution that seemed like something out of a sci-fi movie.

"Is there anything specific that you are looking for?" Dr. Stern questioned, pulling back the sheet, exposing the unfinished work of his staff. Mitchell and I both recoiled at what we saw. "My apologies, as I stated earlier, I am just getting back in the office. I would usually have stitched her up by now, but I didn't even know that she was here." He paused his emotions for a young woman that he obviously knew well crept in.

"How well did you know the Seasons?" I wanted to know.

"Howard was a part of the groomsmen in my first marriage, which was way before Amber was born. It was a time that we were real close, that was until they started doing reality television. It made being friends hard with cameras around knowingly and unknowingly at times."

"I couldn't imagine what that would be like," I responded, being honest. Dr. Stern retrieved some latex gloves and handed each of us a pair.

"Do you have a magnifying glass, Doc?" Mitchell questioned, I knew why.

"For?" Dr. Stern wanted to know before entertaining his question.

"Do you see this mark right here?" Mitchell pointed out with his finger. "Well, I need to get a close look at it."

Dr. Stern released an exasperated sigh before walking to the cabinet that was full of supplies that needed to be used.

"Will this do?" he questioned, as he handed Mitchell and I a pair of glasses with two magnifying lens extensions that could be adjusted.

I placed on the awkward spectacles then leaned in to examine the small teardrop shape etched into her face. I remembered what June had said about the ritual that frats used on freshmen to brand them. I studied the odd shape more, and I could tell that it was done with something that would maintain the shape, but the skin is not bruised like it would be if a tattoo had been performed. This left me confused, as to how it was applied to her face, and what the heck did it mean.

"Dr. Stern, this mark is very peculiar and is not something our victim had on her face before her abduction. What have you come across over the years that would cause a mark like this, without causing much damage to the skin under it?" I asked, as I removed the magnifying specs that he'd given me, and handed them to him.

Dr. Stern removed his glasses before placing the odd specs onto his face. He adjusted the lenses accordingly, mumbling to himself as he did so. After about a minute of incoherent words, he lifted his head and removed the specs.

"That peculiar mark was caused post mortem, which is why the skin surrounding it is not damaged. There was also some sort of adhesive applied there. I'm still not sure what was used to cause this. Why is this mark so important? It had nothing to do with the cause of death," he concluded

"Maybe not, but I have a feeling it was placed there for a reason, and I plan to find out how and why," I told him. "Can you have someone take a look at that closer, I just want to be sure that it was placed on after death, which says a lot about our killers."

"What does it say? I'm curious," Dr. Stern questioned

"It lets us know that they are patient, have plenty of time on their hands to be so meticulous, and one more thing."

"What's that?" Mitchell fell into my rationale as well, urging me to conclude.

"They don't want to be caught, as they make their point, which is scary," I added

CHAPTER TWENTY

MISSY

I made it back to the mansion just before 5 a.m. I saw that Daphne had made it back safe. I made sure that no one could see me, before making my way inside. Once inside, I hurried to Daphne's room. Her door was locked, so I tapped lightly on the door, and she didn't respond. I pulled my blade out of my pocket and forced open the door. I saw the bathroom light on and proceeded in that direction.

Daphne was sitting on the bathroom floor, naked, with her gun in her hand. "Hey, Daphne, are you okay?"

Daphne jumped up off the floor and pointed her gun at me. I threw my hands up, and backed up to the bathroom door, closing us in. "What the fuck did you make me do Catherine? Who are you?" She was yelling at the top of her lungs.

"Daphne, you need to calm down…stop yelling before you wake Gramma up, and she sees what's going on. Put the gun down, and I'll explain everything, please." I kept my distance, and I knew that she was still in shock and pulling that trigger by mistake could easily happen.

"You fucking liar…you manipulated me as you alway have." She was extremely loud, and I couldn't risk someone coming in to check on her.

"Look, you and I know that you aren't going to shoot me. If you feel bad about it, call the police right now and turn me in. I'll tell them what I did, and leave you out of it." I could tell that she was considering making that call, as the tension in her arms eased slightly. "You had nothing to do with what happened, and don't worry, I burned the place down so it's as if you were never there. The only people that know about this are you and I," I honestly told her.

Daphne lowered the gun down to her side, then collapsed back down to the floor, tears racing down her cheeks. I rushed over to her, removed the gun from her hand, and sat it on the sink counter, then I placed my arms around her.

"It's okay Sis, it's okay," I whispered to her.

"It's not…I killed someone. I can't take that back." She was right. I didn't know what to tell her, as killing came easy to me.

"I know it's hard, but in some situations you have no choice. Brent was trying to hurt us, whether physically or emotionally, it was his intent. He had video recording equipment set up throughout the house, even in the bathroom.

Daphne had now stopped crying, and lifted her head to face me. "That still doesn't mean he deserved to die," she reasoned.

"I didn't say that, but who knows where those videos go, and that last thing I would want is for Gramma to hear about us on the internet in compromising ways." I played on her love for Gramma.

Daphne removed my arm from around her then stood up. I made sure to pick up the gun before she did and placed it in my waist. I was still covered with blood, and I knew that people would be moving around soon and looking for us.

"The family will be up soon and looking for us to join them for breakfast. I need you to be okay. No one can know what happened… you do know that, right?"

Daphne walked over to the tub and sat down and ran her hands through her hair. "I'm going to ask you something Missy, and I want you to be honest with me. Can you do that?"

"Come on, we don't have time for this."

"If you want me to keep this between you and I, then I need you to answer the question." She was serious.

"Go ahead, ask me," I told her, wanting to get cleaned up.

"Is this your first time killing someone?" I wasn't caught off guard by her question, but I said nothing. "The rage in which you attacked that guy was like you were someone else. And now you stand here in dried blood, smelling like smoke, and you are as calm as you can be."

"What do you want me to say, Daphne, that I'm a psychopathic killer? I'm not sure if that's what you're thinking, but I'm not. Have I had to hurt someone, of course, but in this situation, Brent was videoing us without our consent. He was a large man that was under the influence of alcohol and drugs, and it was telling what he was going to do after he finished with us. I do feel bad for Nadia, as she seemed like a good person, but we couldn't take the chance of her not saying anything. You and I are sisters, I trust you, and I would never do anything to hurt you or put you at risk. I would hope that you would do the same for me. All we have left is us and Gramma." I wanted to trust Daphne, but it was up to her what happened from here. "I answered your question, now what?"

Daphne stood, then walked over to me. I took a step back, not knowing what she was about to do.

"We don't have much time to get you cleaned up and ready for breakfast. Your hair is a mess." She raked her hand through my blood stained hair. "I'll grab your things while you bathe. I want you to know that I won't ever say anything about what happened. I will always have your back, Missy, whether you believe that or not." I felt her honesty.

It had been a long time since I felt the wave of emotions that I was feeling now. I regretted having involved Daphne in what took place. In her mind, she was okay after taking someone's life, but in reality, it can weigh on you. I have become numb to any feeling or emotion when it comes to dealing with death, but that's not what I wanted for her.

"Daphne, look at me." I wanted her to understand what I was about to say to her. She made eye contact with me, and I scraped a piece of dried blood off my eyelash before continuing. "What you did tonight will probably eat at you for the next couple of days, weeks, or even years. You will probably find yourself watching tv, reading a book, or on a date when the thought of what you did surfaces. Right now, you are making a decision to live with this, which means you can't address this in therapy, church, or with someone that you feel you trust. Do you understand what I'm saying to you?" I wanted her to know exactly what she was agreeing to.

"Are we going to keep going over the same thing, or can I go get your things?" I smiled and shook my head. I could attest that Daphne had taken her first kill better than I had, if it was indeed her first.

CHAPTER TWENTY-ONE
DETECTIVE LANE

I sat at my desk early Monday morning going over the Seasons' case in my head. I glanced back to see Mitchell sitting across from me, balling up blank pieces of paper and shooting them into the wastebasket. It was his routine whenever he was in deep thought about something.

The facts about this case were starting to hit close to home, and I couldn't help but think about June, and how she's running around the city clueless that young women are being targeted. My thoughts were interrupted by the ringing of my desk phone.

The person didn't give me a chance to say hello as they began with a question. "Is this Detective Lane?" a female's deep voice spoke over the line.

"Yes it is, can I ask who I am speaking with?" Mitchell's head swung in my direction, I was hoping that it was a lead.

"Yes, this is Agent Lizzy Mae from the GBI, and I hear you have a case that you need help with."

That was fast I thought to myself, and I held down the phone and let Mitchell know who I was speaking with. "Thanks for calling."

"You're absolutely welcome. I have been working cases such as the one you're now on for over thirty years. I do know that we have a lot of resources that you guys don't, so even if you just need help in that capacity, I'm willing to do what I can."

I was astonished that the GBI would provide an agent to come over to lend me their expertise. It's something that I wasn't turning down. I jumped at the opportunity that Agent Lizzie May had given me. "That would be great, Special Agent Mae, we need all the help that we can get. How soon can we meet up?" I was ready to get these files in front of her and see what she thought about a case that had no physical evidence.

"We can meet this afternoon, if that's okay with you. I'm just cleaning out my desk as we speak," she told me.

"Cleaning out your desk…for the day?"

"No honey, I've been doing this law enforcement thing too long; I have grandkids now, so I'm retiring. I have an opportunity to spend time with them, unlike when my children were growing up. So, I guess this is your lucky day, being that you are technically my last assignment." She sounded ecstatic, and I was happy for her.

For an officer to fulfill their career and retire was a major accomplishment. Officers put their lives on the line and are at risk pretty much their entire career when they commit to the shield. I, for one, couldn't wait until the time for me to retire came. " Sounds great, I can't wait. Like my granny used to say 'I'm not one to look a gift horse in the mouth'. I'll see you this afternoon, Special agent Mae."

She said her goodbye and disconnected.

"Mitchell, we need to be heading out. We're scheduled to meet Special Agent Mae in Decatur soon, and I want to make a stop before we do," I told him. Mitchell peered across his cluttered desk at me like I just asked him to work overtime.

"Who is Special agent Mae?"

"Special Agent Mae is a profiler for GBI She is on her way into retirement, and she has been assigned to provide help in these killings any way needed. I mean at this point, we need all hands on deck, wouldn't you agree?"

Something was up with Mitchell, and I couldn't put my finger on it. The shooting of the balled up paper was the first indicator. "Lane, would you mind taking the meeting with the agent by yourself? I think I'll pass on this meeting, I have a personal matter that I need to handle. I think that you and I need to be going over this case before we let some other set of eyes in."

"Are you serious right now, Mitchell? I'm sitting here with the file right in front of me, while you've been over there tossing balled up paper in the trash for the last ten minutes." I didn't want to call him out, but his personal life was starting to be an issue every other week.

"This is how I gather my thoughts, and you know that, Lane. But yeah, I need to handle some things, and we can catch up later, if that's ok with you." Mitchell looked exhausted. Neither of us had dealt with a case like this before, and it was obvious that it was taking its toll on him.

"Sure, not a problem Mitchell, but there's one thing that I need you to understand, and that is, this case won't be solved quickly. We have to keep our wits about us, and continue to work as a team. We can't keep secrets from each other, move recklessly, or let what is going on in our personal lives interfere in this case. Now that the G.B.I are coming on board, we should be able to make some headway. Take what you need home with you, and try to get some rest, and come back tomorrow refreshed and ready to get at it again," I suggested, hoping Mitchell would take the offer.

Mitchell gave me half a smile then nodded. "Yeah, maybe you're right. Rest sounds like a great idea. Call me if you need me, Lane," he replied, slowly gathering his things.

I gathered my things knowing that I wouldn't be returning to the office after my meeting with Special Agent Mae. Mitchell and I walked to our vehicles in silence before saying our goodbyes.

Once I was in my car, I pulled out my cell phone to verify the address that Special Agent Mae had texted me. Jerry Yum's Wings on Candler Road was my destination, and I knew exactly where the wing hub was. I had never been there, but it was a well known establishment in town and not far from G.B.I Headquarters. The drive would take thirty minutes, but I wasn't in the mood for any music, so I rode in silence letting my mind wander as it wished.

I pulled into the small parking lot that shared space with a tattoo parlor. There was a small crowd outside. The people inhaled and exhaled smoke as they conversed. With a series of vibrations, my phone notified me that I had a text message.

> Go inside and find us a table near the door.
> I'll be there shortly, I'm walking out now.

I responded to Special Agent Mae with a simple "Okay" and got out of my car. Looking around at the small crowd that was now down to three males and one female, I locked my door and slung my purse over my shoulder, heading into the restaurant. I could hear the catcalls from behind me.

"Hey, Ms. Officer. Shawty got a walk on her. Let me show you how to work those handcuffs later," were a few choice words that I managed to hear, but I didn't entertain their childish behavior.

I made my way into the restaurant and surveyed the place. The food smelled delicious. There was a couple placing an order and a few other patrons waiting patiently as if still deciding on their selection. I made my way to a booth that was not far from the side door, and took a seat, removing some bleach wipes from my purse. I began wiping the table down. Walking to the trash bin to throw the wipes away, I bumped into a woman who was entering.

"I'm so sorry for bumping into you."

"It's okay." I recognized her voice instantly.

"Special Agent Mae?" I questioned.

She smiled then extended her hand. "That would be me." I wore a look of surprise as she was not what I had envisioned upon speaking with her. I had pictured a Caucasian woman, born in the deep south due to her accent, and presumably middle aged. Boy, was I wrong.

Before me stood a woman taller than myself, at least five foot ten inches tall. Her two piece business suit hugged the curves on her athletic frame. Her hair was pulled back into a long ponytail that contained a few gray strands which enhanced her beauty. I'm sure if she had not chosen law enforcement, she could've been a model. I finally let her hand go, and she maintained her smile as I led her to our booth.

"You don't look like what I expected, and I mean that in a good way," I told her, as she was beautiful, and did an awesome job of maintaining her body over the years.

"I get that most of the time when I first meet someone after speaking to them over the phone. I like to dress nice, and I can't do that being out of shape," she added.

"I wish I had your discipline, but you are right, Special Agent Mae. It's funny that you say you get that confusion all the time about your age, do you think it's based on your voice? I mean you do sound like a country Caucasian woman, to say the least," I confessed

"It most certainly does, I'm sure of it. But, I'm just a country farm girl raised in Virginia by my adopted parents that happened to be white," she stated matter-of-factly. "Lets order our food then we can talk, is that okay? By the way, lunch is on me, and that's not up for debate," she claimed.

We walked to the counter and placed our order. I could smell the oily food being cooked to order. We let a couple in front of us order, then we did the same. I ordered honey hot wings with shrimp fried rice and a large Sprite. Special Agent Mae ordered lemon pepper wings, fries, a small vegetable fried rice, and a lemonade fruit punch mix to drink, and to think her body still looked amazing.

It didn't take long before our food was being handed to us. We walked around and found a table near the door. Special Agent Mae removed some hand sanitizer from her purse, offered me some, then returned it back to her bag. She didn't wait for me, as she bowed her head and said her prayers. I couldn't keep my eyes off of her, until she started placing napkins on her lap and looked up at me.

"Is everything alright?" she asked me

"Yes, I was about to pray as well," I lied, but I lowered my head to pray. When I pulled it back up, Special Agent Mae had a french fry half way in her mouth, staring at me with curiosity.

When she didn't break her gaze, I had to question her. "Is everything alright, Special Agent Mae?" I posed her question back. She smiled, took a sip of her drink then nodded.

"Everythings fine, and please call me Lizzy Mae, which is my first and middle name. I'm retiring soon, and I want to get used to hearing it."

"Okay, Lizzy Mae it is. First off, thank you for agreeing to assist us with this case, especially with you on your way out the door. Upon speaking with you earlier, I noticed in the email that you sent me, that you weren't the original officer assigned to assist us," I told her, wishing that Mitchell had joined us.

"Yes, there was a younger, more vibrant agent assigned, but I didn't think she had the experience, or the people skills, to deal with something like this just yet, if you know what I mean." I didn't, but I played along.

"Well, thank you. On behalf of APD, we are grateful for all the assistance we can get being that this case could get a lot of publicity, and quickly."

"You're right, and you're welcome. To be honest, I love these types of cases. Over the course of my career, I managed to help catch and convict five serial killers and over a dozen serial rapists. Can you tell me what you have so far when it comes to evidence?" she questioned.

"As far as evidence, we have nothing. No trace fibers, nothing in the way of toxicology, and no motive. We do know that each of the victims were college students who came from affluent families. I've factored that in as evidence. Also, the bodies of each woman reeked of bleach, and their eyes have been removed. I made a copy of the file we have for you to take with you, as well as the photos of our victims and crime scene–the dump locations."

"Great, I see that you are on top of things. So, Tracy... Can I call you Tracy?"

"I guess, I mean of course, why not?" I replied.

"Don't worry, I will do so only when we're alone. If we're going to be working together, I need you to trust me. This is your case, but I have the experience and the resources. I won't divulge any information to the media, coworkers, or family members for that matter. I'll provide updates to my supervisors only when necessary, and I would like you to do the same.

"In this field, you have to realize that as officers we have a common goal at times, but there are some who care about pleasing the brass at the top. The brass at the top only care about the end result, meaning it's the people working with you that can hinder you. Be very careful with what you share, and trust your skills that have gotten you to where you are in your career." She shared some words of wisdom with me.

"Thank you for those words of advice."

"No problem. Now, you mentioned that this will soon be a high profile case, which means your superiors will be hard pressed for answers and updates."

"They already are," I confessed

"That's okay. Now that G.B.I is involved, you can refer them to me. I can handle their pressure a lot better than you can, that way you're in the clear," she offered, while eating another spoon full of fried rice. She had a look of concern on her face for me. "Hey, don't worry yourself much, you hear me? We'll get this thing solved. We just have our work cut out for us, but that's to be expected."

"I hope so," I replied, relieved that at least someone was confident.

"Believe me when I tell you that I'm one of the best profilers there is. I can look at someone and tell you almost any and everything about them."

"Oh really?" I questioned, not doubting her skill, but not fully believing her statement either.

Lizzie Mae took another sip of her drink. "Let's put it to a test then. Do you mind if I use you for my example?"

"Sure, why not. Just be prepared to hear the truth if your profile of me is off when you're done," I let her know.

Lizzy Mae sat her cup down then stared at me as if she was looking right through me. She began rubbing her chin in deep thought before she smiled. "Let us begin. You, Tracy Lane, are a self-imposed introvert. Before becoming an officer you loved to mingle and enjoy people you considered to be friends. That all changed as now you don't trust people, other than your family. Even so, you can't trust them much due to their worldly activities…"

She raised her eyebrows and nodded. "…because it goes against what you do for a living. You decided to become a cop, not out of wanting to protect and serve but to protect yourself. You have always attracted the wrong men, as was the case early in your law enforcement career. Your beauty overshadowed your skills as an officer, and someone took advantage of that."

I adjusted in my seat. "Go on," I stated.

"Since then, you've felt the need to constantly isolate yourself and immerse yourself in your work. You're an overthinker which allows you to pay attention to the small details, but it's a cancer for your love life." Again, I adjusted and smiled nervously.

"That's very interesting," I stated.

"I'm not done," she stated to my surprise. "You are also overprotective, which is why your daughter chose to leave the city to go to college. Now, I'm done," she stated boastfully.

"Good. Because if I hear anymore, I'd think you have taken up residence in my head. And I'm not overprotective, I'm just a concerned mother with an eagerness to be an independent child," I said in my defense.

We both laughed. "Okay, Tracy, I hear you. What time do you usually arrive at the office?" she questioned.

"No later than eight in the morning most days."

"Great. I usually finish my workout around seven, so I'll meet you at your office and hopefully, your partner is well rested," she stated, giving me a wink.

"What? How? Nevermind." I was amazed.

I thanked her for lunch, and we gathered our leftovers before she walked me to my car. The same characters stood outside the tattoo parlor, but no one uttered a word, to my surprise.

"Don't be shy now fellas," Lizzy Mae stated. Their reply was a simple wave with no words. "I'm well known around these parts." Her country accent was strong. "They didn't bother you, did they?"

"No, not at all," I lied.

"Good. I'll see you tomorrow then," she stated, then surprised me when she reached out and gave me a hug. "I'm a hugger at times." She smiled a warm smile, and I returned her embrace before getting inside my car.

I drove home in silence the same way I had driven to the restaurant. My mind was on the lunch date with Lizzy Mae. Now that I've spoken to her, I now look forward to working and learning from her. Solving this case with her was going to be the uplifting event that I now needed in my life.

CHAPTER TWENTY-TWO
DETECTIVE LANE

"Mom, do you want butter on the popcorn or not?"

"What did you say, June?" I was flipping through the autopsy report of Amber Seasons.

"Come on, Mom. I've been here two days, and we finally get a night for us to hang out, and you could care less. You're still caught up in your work!" June expressed to me as she peeked her head out of the kitchen.

I sat down the file that had consumed my thoughts daily. I knew that I was overlooking something, but I couldn't figure out what it was. "Hey baby, I apologize. I am shutting it down." I walked into the kitchen to where she was pulling the second bag of popcorn out of the microwave. I had totally forgotten about our movie night.

I grabbed a bowl for my popcorn, then two bottled waters out of the fridge. June poured the fresh popped corn into each of our bowls, then added butter to hers only. "You don't need any butter, Mom," she advised me

"And you do? I want you around too," I shot back, then placed my hand on her shoulder in a show of affection. I stroked her hair, then smiled as I admired her beauty.

June loved it when I treated her like she was still a little girl. Her father had never been in her life, so I made sure that she always knew that she was at the center of my world. I got lost in trying to establish my career, and our relationship took a hit because of it. My schedule was hectic, and early on, I didn't know at the time how to balance my life.

"Is everything alright, Mom? I can tell that something is weighing on you." She stepped away from me, so that I couldn't rub her anymore, then placed her back against the stove. "Mom, I know you, just like you know me, and I can tell that something is bothering you. Is there something that you want or need to tell me?" She was my mini me in every way.

"Of course, why would you ask me that?"

"If that's the story that you want to stick to, then let's go find a movie, but just know, that I know better."

There wasn't any sense in me hiding my feelings when it came to this case and my feelings for June's safety while on spring break. The one thing that I didn't want to do was scare her, but the fact of the matter was, this was a scary situation. There are people out here killing young women, and just because she didn't fit the profile of the victims, didn't mean that she was excluded.

Killers love the thrill of killing, just like a chef loves to cook, which means the meal doesn't matter. It could easily be a young African American athlete in the headlines next week turning up dead, in the same way, and she needed to know that.

I took a deep breath before I began. I asked her to follow me into the living room, where we could sit down. I picked up the file from the table and placed it on my lap. "You are right, I know you, and you obviously know me very well. Over the past month we have had a couple of young women come up missing."

"That's not uncommon, especially here in Atlanta, where sex trafficking is high."

"I know that, June, just listen. This is different, in that these people aren't taking people to make them slaves, they are taking young women to kill and put out for display for the world to see." I could see the shock on her face.

"Do you guys have any idea who's doing this?"

"We don't, and as of now, they haven't left any evidence. I'm not speaking to you about this to scare you, but for you to be more aware. Something doesn't sit right with me when it comes to this case, and I think these young women are just the beginning of something terrible to come."

June placed her hand on my lap, mistakenly knocking the file to the floor. A photo of Amber Seasons from the neck up fell out from the day that she was discovered. She was like a beautiful human porcelain doll, except the cartoonish eyes that mocked her very existence.

"What is this, Mom? Why did they do this to her?" June asked me, as she picked the file up off the floor and handed it to me. She stared at the photo briefly before giving it to me.

"That is what I intend to find out. As of now, the women have been Caucasian women athletes." I didn't add that they were from wealthy families, as it might have no bearing. I do know that they don't want to be caught, as they have left no evidence, and cleaned the bodies with bleach before dumping them. I can't go into too much in detail, but this is what has been on my mind."

"I appreciate you telling me, not just for my sake, but for yours as well, Mom. You're a worry box, and I know that thinking about me will affect you doing your job well, as it has happened in the past. I assure you that I will be more aware of my surroundings, and while I'm here, I won't be traveling around alone unless I have no choice. I am still sharing my location with you, and I keep my weapon with me; there's not anything more that you nor I can do to make sure I'm safe." She was right, but now that I had done my part by making her aware of what was bothering me, and what was going on in this city, I felt better.

"You have a point, but I will be concerned about you until I can't be, June. Enough about work, go ahead and find something for us to watch, while I go get our drinks." I got up to head to the kitchen when I heard her ask.

"Crime thriller?" I gave her a knowing look, and she burst out laughing. "Kidding, Mom."

"I'm sure you are…you're hilarious."

CHAPTER TWENTY-THREE
DETECTIVE LANE

fter two days of not hearing a word from the alphabet crew, consisting of the F.B.I, and GBI, I was excited when patrol officers brought two suspects in for auto theft. During the intake of their property, it was discovered that a personal item from our case was discovered. I was told that it was a male in one interrogation.

We got off the elevator with notepads in hand, not knowing what to expect. Could it be this easy that our killers had somehow got caught in the midst of stealing a car? I doubted it. We walked down the narrow hallway and were greeted by a handful of patrol officers and detectives mulling around both interrogation rooms, also wondering if we had indeed lucked out and apprehended our suspects.

"Good morning, fellas," Mitchell greeted them with handshakes.

I simply spoke and let Mitchell handle the conversation. "So, what do we know about them?"

One of the officers handed Mitchell two folders, each of them had a dated mugshot attached to it. Mitchell handed me the one with the female's name on it.

"Brian and Heather…doesn't have a ring to it, does it?" one of the officers commented.

I thought about the question that he had just posed. It didn't have a ring to it at all, but how they came into our victims' property was all that mattered at the moment. I did know for a fact that the people we were looking for did not have a criminal record. The vehicle would make killing and transporting the bodies around extremely hard, due worrying about getting their name run, if pulled over.

"Mitchell, let's get this over with," I told him, already knowing these weren't our guys.

"Cool, I'll talk to the male in room one, and you talk to the female in two," Mitchell suggested.

"No, I'll talk to him," I stated firmly. Mitchell shrugged his shoulders and walked into room two. I adjusted my pantsuit, then walked into the room.

I walked in to see a young man sitting, with one hand cuffed to the steel bar attached to the desk, and his other arm folded into his body as if he was cold. His hair was red and ruffled, and he had matching freckles. He still reeked of cigarettes and looked as if he stayed on the go, barely changing clothes. He was apprehended with a book bag with clothing inside.

He tracked my every move as I pulled out my chair. He was large in stature with giant hands. His face registered confusion, and I knew what his next question would be.

"Who the fuck are you?" I ignored his comment. He wore a menacing scowl on his face that I was sure some found intimidating. I took my time in scanning over his file briefly before speaking.

"Brian, I was assured that you were read your Miranda rights, is that right?" He nodded. "Can you please use your words?"

"What the fuck am I being held for?"

"I'm asking the questions, and I'm waiting for you to answer the first question so that we may begin."

"Yeah, I was read my fucking rights, you think I'd be sitting in here if they didn't?" He wanted this to be hard, I could tell.

"Do you know why you are here, Mr. Smith?" He shook his head no.

"Mr. Smith, the recorder can't deduce your answer, so once again, I need you to use your words. This can go however you want, and right now, you're trending in the wrong direction." He knew I was serious as he adjusted himself upright and answered my question.

"No. No, I don't know why I'm here. I know that Heather and I were getting off work when the police came at us out of nowhere, like we were Bonnie and Clyde, then took us into custody." I brushed off his over-dramatization.

I didn't have time for the clueless act. "How did you come into possession of the property of Amber Seasons?"

"Who?"

"Amber Seasons. Does that name sound familiar?"

He hesitated before replying, "I don't know who that is." Then turned his head away from me. I could tell the tough guy act was back.

I stood then walked over to the two-way mirror that I was sure had eyes peering through at us and leaned upon it.

"You know Brian… Can I call you Brian? Mr. Smith seems too formal for a guy such as yourself."

His face softened. "Brian is cool."

"Good. You see, Brian. I don't believe in coincidences, do you?" I didn't wait for a reply. "I find it hard to believe that you wouldn't know someone that frequents your store. I find it less of a coincidence that your fingerprints would be on that person's car, especially since you claim you don't know them."

He adjusted his body nervously. A bead of sweat formed on his brow. "I don't know what you're talking about.

"You're starting to sweat, you seemed like you were cold when I walked in. Is the temperature too high?" I knew my questions were starting to bother him, but why I didn't know. "Do you need something to drink or a glass of water?"

"Yes, ma'am, thank you." It was the first time he had acted as if he had manners since I walked in.

The door opened less than a minute later and a uniformed officer handed me two Sprites. I gave Brian one, and he quickly took two gulps, finishing off the bottle.

"Thanks," he stated genuinely. He was no longer sweating.

"As I was about to inform you earlier, Brian, your fingerprints were found on Amber Seasons' car. I see here that you are an employee of GameChangers Sporting Goods and with that, I'm positive that you have seen her at some point or another, as she was a frequent customer. This is a homicide investigation, so if you are hiding something, then I suggest you come up with it right now." Brian peered at the two-way glass then finished the rest of his soda. He ran his left hand through his matted hair, shaking it as he stroked it in despair.

"It was all Heather's idea," he mumbled.

"Speak up, Brian."

He lifted his head. "It was Heather's idea."

"What was Heather's idea?" I questioned, wondering if I had eliminated Brian and Heather as a suspect prematurely? Although Brian was wearing leg restraints, he was a large man that looked very agile, so I positioned myself closer to the door as I urged him to continue on.

"Heather told me that she noticed a car that had been in the parking lot for a few days. She told me that she saw a purse under the front seat. So one day, when we got off work, I went with her to check it out."

"Hold it, Brian. If you think I'm going to stand here and let you feed me a bullshit story like this, you're sadly mistaken."

"It's the truth! We went to her car, and I saw the straps of the purse under the passenger seat. I opened the door and took it out. Heather popped the trunk, but there was nothing worth taking, so we locked it up, then left."

"So the car was unlocked?"

"No, I unlocked it. I used to know how to get into locked cars."

"You mean you used to break into cars." I walked over and picked up his file. "Joyriding, reduced from grand theft, only because it was your uncle's car that you stole. What did you do with the purse and the contents in it?" I knew that it was a small chance of them still having it, since it wasn't in the property they were arrested with.

"Heather has the purse, and we still have most of the money and the credit cards we didn't use."

"Is there a reason that you didn't use the cards and get rid of them?" I wanted to know the logic behind keeping that kind of evidence, if you weren't going to use it.

He looked me in the eyes, and I could see a tinge of regret. I wasn't surprised when he began speaking his truth.

"I knew her. I didn't know we had broken into her car or that she was missing until we watched the news. Heather suggested that we put the stuff back in the car, but by the time we decided to, it was gone. I hate to hear what happened to her, but if you think that we had something to do with that, you're mistaken."

"I'm not the one who made a mistake, Brian. Have a good day," I told him, then knocked on the door to be let out.

I was met outside by Lt. Johnson, to my surprise, upon my exit.

"What are you doing, Lane?" He questioned through gritted teeth to where only I could hear, as others were standing around.

"What does it look like…my job?"

"You know exactly what I mean, you just ended that interview abruptly. You don't know what else he knows."

I looked at Lt. Johnson in disbelief. It was taking everything in my power to force a smile as I said what I needed to say. "You asked me to report to you when I have something right?" He nodded "The person that we have in there is what he should be in there for, and that's for theft. Neither of them are killers, nor do they have any information that will help us catch these killers. You're to go in there and continue a conversation with him if you want. I left an unopened Sprite on the table you can have too," I said before walking to where Mitchell was.

Before I was let in the door of the interrogation room, Mitchell walked out. "Waste of time," we said in unison. We laughed, then walked off to where we could speak in private, as eyes stayed glued to us.

"What's up Lane, did you get anything useful, besides a spontaneous theft opportunity happening here? Brian had said that the car was there for several days before they broke into it, according to him anyway."

"She said the same thing before excluding herself from any participation in breaking into the car. Do you believe them?" he asked.

"They're barely out of their teens, maybe 24, with misdemeanors on their records. They aren't who we are looking for. He admitted that he knew who she was, and that she was a nice person, which we already have heard several times. "

"Yeah, I didn't think so either. It's always the nice ones that get taken out," Mictchell added for no apparent reason "So, what now?"

"I think we need to speak back with the manager at the sporting goods store. Let's head back to the desk, there's too many ears around."

Mitchell and I made it back to our desk and exchanged notes from our interviews. "We need to contact Mark, and verify some things," I let Michell know.

"I have his card here. He put the phone on speaker, then dialed the number.

"GameChangers, this is Mark, how may I help you?"

"Hey Mark, this is Detective Mitchell. We needed to come review some video footage, is that okay?"

"What,do you mean? Right now?"

"Is that a problem?"

"I mean, I don't want that kind of attention here at the store."

"You don't want the kind of attention that you would receive for not cooperating in an active investigation," I made him aware.

"Okay, okay...does this have anything to do with Heather and Brian?"

"It does."

"I knew that boy was trouble. Yeah, sure, I'll be awaiting your arrival."

"Thanks Mark, we'll be there shortly." Mitchell ended the call, then signaled for a uniformed officer. Mitchell and I made it to the massive sporting goods store, and Mark was waiting at the entrance looking flustered.

"Hey, come on in." He led us through the store at a fast pace, as if he was sneaking us in. I chose not to address it, as he had already stated that he was uncomfortable with us coming. "You don't think they're responsible for the missing girl, do you?" Mark questioned as we approached the office door.

"Not missing, murdered," Mitchell corrected.

Mark's face registered shock. He fumbled with the store keys before unlocking the door and leading us inside. The store was dimly lit. The emergency exit signs and auxiliary lights provided the only means of illumination. Mark led us to the same dark room we'd visited weeks earlier.

"What exactly are we looking for?" the security officer questioned typing in his password.

"Pull up the security footage of the parking lot from April 5th through April 14th," I told him. "Go slow, please."

The video tech went through each day frame by frame. Tuesday, Wednesday, Thursday, Friday, Saturday, then Sunday.

"Hold it, stop it right there," I yelled. "Right there, there's…"

"Heather," Mark finished my sentence. "What is she doing?"

Heather was standing in the middle of the empty parking lot with her hands in her pants pocket. She was there on the day the store was closed, which was on a Sunday. Her hair was pulled back into a pony-tail that flowed out the back of the Atlanta Braves baseball cap she wore. She looked in both directions cautiously as if she were about to cross into a traffic-laden street. Moments later, a male appeared wearing a hooded sweatshirt.

"That's Brian. I can tell by his walk," Mark confirmed for us.

The pair walked slowly, each surveying their surroundings with every step. Amber Seasons' car came into view.

"Why didn' this footage show up last time that we were here?" I questioned, although we could barely see the car.

"We didn't pull up these dates, that's why," the video attendant mouthed snidely.

"Hey, do your job and stop with the smart remarks," Mark straightened him out.

The duo stopped suddenly before engaging in a brief conversation that seemed to get heated. It appeared that one was trying to persuade the other about something. Apparently, Brian had gotten cold feet because Heather threw her hands up dismissively before continuing her trek towards the abandoned vehicle. Then, the footage cutoff.

"What happened?" Mitchell questioned.

"That's it. That's as far as the footage goes, and the camera's view," Mark informed us.

"Fuck! At least this confirms their story. I wanted to see if there was any evidence left around near the car from the abduction, but I highly doubt there was any."

"This is un-fucking-believable!" Mark sounded angry "You can bet your ass that they're both fired!"

"That's your call, Mark. Can you make us a copy like you did before?" was my only concern.

"Sure, can you give me ten minutes?" he replied.

"Mitchell," I called out to him as I headed out the door.

"What's up, Lane?"

"The video we just saw corroborated their story about breaking into the car. We will keep the video as evidence, but there's nothing there."

"That doesn't necessarily eliminate them as our murder suspects though. They could have been markers, like they are used in sex trafficking."

"You may be right, but did you see how they moved? Heather and Brian are two kids that couldn't even agree on doing a simple B and E. Imagine if they tried to commit murder together. The suspects that we're looking for are very meticulous. These kids knew the store had cameras because they worked here, and they still went through with their plan. There is no way the people we are looking for would be that crazy."

"You have a point. So what now?"

"For now, we secure the tape and get some rest before we get back at it tomorrow."

"In other words, we're back at square one," Mitchell retorted.

"Try not to look at the glass as half empty all the time," I stated before going back inside to secure the tape.

We headed back to the station and signed the video in as evidence.

The Seasons were at the property desk, picking up their daughter's items that we were told we couldn't hold. They decided not to press charges on Heather and Brian, saying that the loss of their child was enough to deal with. I couldn't blame them. Mitchell and I had done enough for the day, so after making a few more calls, I headed home.

CHAPTER TWENTY-FOUR
DETECTIVE LANE

I made it to the house around 6 p.m., and June was asleep on the couch. I shut the TV off, went and retrieved a comforter, then placed the large, warm cover over the both of us. Before long, I was asleep, returning to a nightmare I wish I could forget.

"I call my next witness, Detective Lane, to the stand." I walked to the stand slowly, and glanced at the defendant whose sinister look had me wishing that things had turned out differently than they did. After being sworn in, I gave my attention to the defense attorney.

"Detective, could you please tell us your name, title, and how long you've been on the force?"

"My name is Detective Tracy Lane. I'm a homicide detective for the Atlanta Police Department., and I've been on the force for fifteen years."

From there I proceeded to answer questions from the defense as if I were the one on trial. For fifteen minutes, I was forced to maintain my composure as the defense did everything they could to discredit me.

"Detective Lane, is it safe to say that had your fellow officers not intervened as you tried to apprehend Mr. Gamble, that you would have killed him in cold blood?" The defense counsel challenged my rationale while out in the field.

"*Objection, your Honor. The relevance of that question has nothing to do with the fact that Mr. Gamble wasn't killed in cold blood,*" *the prosecution blurted out.*

"*Objection sustained, Counsel,*" *the judge said sternly.*

I looked at Gamble, and he winked. I looked at the judge, and it was obvious that I was the only one who witnessed it.

"*Detective Lane, in your own words, tell us what happened two years ago, when you and your partner were in pursuit of Mr. Gamble. A pursuit that resulted in your partner's untimely demise,*" *he added for no reason, and it was said with no emotion.* "*And, please don't leave anything out.*"

I closed my eyes, then took several deep breaths before opening my eyes and speaking.

2 YEARS AGO

"*J*ackson! Jackson!*" I yelled as he jumped out of our vehicle in pursuit of Johnny Gamble, a murder suspect, as I radioed for backup. I exited the vehicle and was following Jackson's direction. I knew that Johnny Gamble was wanted for multiple homicides and was labeled armed and dangerous. He led us on a chase into an area full of warehouses near the pier. I remembered that it was a humid night, and the moon partly hid behind the clouds.*

I walked slowly with my weapon clutched to my chest, prepared for any and everything. My heart raced with fear, and I could feel my hands shaking. I wanted to call Jackson over the radio, but given the situation, I would possibly be giving away his location, so I passed. The little light that was being shone by the moon had now been covered, and all I saw was shadows. I pulled out my flashlight and held it out in front of me with my weapon pointed in the same direction.

I took a step after I kicked something on the ground. I pointed the flashlight to see what it was and saw that it was Jackson's radio. I secured it to my belt and slowly crept forward. I heard what sounded like a large piece of metal hitting the ground, then shots being fired. I hurried in the direction of the sound and rounded the corner. All I saw was my partner of five years lying face down. I couldn't tell whether he was alive or not, with the way Johnny Gamble was leaning over him. Johnny lifted Jackson's limp body to where he looked as if he were kneeling, and used him as a shield. He held a weapon to the back of Jackson's head.

"Put your weapon down and put your hands up. Back up is on the way. This doesn't have to end badly, Gamble," I urged him, hoping that he would comply.

"Do I look like the type to take orders?" Gamble questioned before stepping back and firing a round into the back of Jackson's skull. I watched in horror as Jackson's head exploded, just as the moonlight came out from behind the clouds. I immediately dropped onto my stomach and fired shots in Gamble's direction. I could hear him laughing. Bullets whisked past me as he returned fire.

I started to hear the faint sound of sirens in the distance and prayed that they would hurry. Bullets hit the ground inches from me, sending pieces of the concrete onto my face. I rolled over to where I was close to the wall and got into a crouching position.

I could make out Johnny's silhouette in the moonlight, and I had a clear shot. I fired two rounds that hit its mark, and I watched him hit the ground with a loud yelp. The sounds of screeching tires barely drowned him out as he continued to yell and curse. The area became lit up like a football field, and swarmed with police.

"This is Detective Lane!" I called out from my position to let them know who I was, so they wouldn't open fire. "He's still armed," I yelled.

I began walking toward him, and I could feel that I had busted my knee up pretty bad. Gamble lay on his back clutching his stomach. SWAT officers crept past me with body armor, as if there was still a threat.

"Check him completely," I ordered and watched as officers rolled him onto his side, exposing his back where another weapon was hidden. "You sonofabitch, I should blow your fucking head off." At that moment, I meant it.

Paramedics rushed past me to check on Jackson and attend to Johnny Gamble. I got up and ran to where Jackson lay face down. I was stopped before I could get to him.

"He's gone," the officer informed me.

I watched as a sheet was placed over my partner, whom I had just had lunch with, and shared a laugh about the department's last softball game. I dropped down to my knee, causing myself pain in the process. I placed my gun in my holster, then placed my hands over my eyes. I thought about how Jackson's twin sons would handle the news, he was their world. His wife, who has just retired from her job, so that she could be there when he got off work, would now be heartbroken. I could not control my emotions anymore. As I stood up, I removed my weapon from my holster.

Johnny Gamble was now on a gurney, bandaged up as best they could until he could make it to a hospital to continue the process of recovering from a gunshot wound. Meanwhile, my partner's lifeless body lay feet away from us. This entire scene was wrong, Gamble should be the one covered up.

"Get away from him," I calmly stated as I placed the gun to his temple.

"Lane! Lane! Put down your weapon. It's not worth it," I heard someone say.

"Do it, bitch!" he encouraged me. His emerald green, bloodshot eyes dared me to end his life. "You scared?" He was ready to die, and I knew it.

I was shaking so bad, but I was intent. I grabbed a handful of his hair forcefully. "Where you're going to end up, you're gonna wish you were dead," I said through clenched teeth, having used every muscle in my body to stop me from pulling the trigger.

"Get him out of here," one of the officers called out as I put my gun back up.

"Lane, you need some help," I heard him say, before I passed out. I didn't know that at the time. I thought I had fallen and busted up my knee, but in fact, I had been shot right above my knee.

CHAPTER TWENTY-FIVE
DETECTIVE LANE

After weeks of meetings and surveillance where college athletes frequented, things remained quiet. We issued out a report by Special Agent Mae that entailed the killer's profile, as well as how they may abduct women. As of now, the FBI had nothing nationally that fit our crimes. In Special Agent Mae's file, she included that a plausible ruse is most likely used to lure the young women into thinking things are safe. She describes the woman suspect as being small, non threatening by her appearance, and would appear normal amongst others. She had no description of the male, other than he was the enforcer, and handler of the victims.

Mitchell and I had just come from our morning meeting when we saw officers moving around in a hurry. "What's going on?" I stopped one officer and questioned. Before he could reply, a call came over Mitchell's radio. He listened intently as a location for us to proceed to was given where another body had been discovered.

"I'll drive," Mitchell volunteered

We sped to the crime scene. There were reporters onsite, scattered about, giving their opening lines. "Good evening, this is Sandy Brown reporting live from…"

"Katy Burly here reporting live from the scene where the body of a female..." I heard a reporter say. I realized that every local news station was being represented.

"Mitchell, get someone on this ASAP," I ordered as we made our way to the crime scene tape.

Mitchell signaled for a couple of uniformed officers.

"Get these reporters back, and set up barriers and privacy screens. We don't want any photos leaked."

"We have a right to report the news!" someone yelled after hearing Mitchell's orders.

"Yeah, you do, but you'll be doing it from over there." He pointed, giving the officers a place to herd them.

I was pleased with the handling of this crime scene. The victim's body had been concealed from the media and public. There were officers mulling around as the sun had just woken up from its slumber. The smell of coffee was strong, as everyone knew that this would be a long day.

"Lane, Mitchell, good to see you," Todd, one of the detectives in our unit greeted us. "Same M.O. A young woman displayed, just like your other victims." He then gave a brief summary.

"Thank you," I replied.

"Let's take a look," Mitchell suggested. An unsettling feeling overcame me as we approached the barrier surrounding the body. Mitchell noticed my apprehension.

"Lane, is everything alright?" he questioned, placing a calming hand on my shoulder. I shook my head no.

This had an eerily familiar feeling to it, and I hoped that my gut feeling was wrong. As the officer held open the screen tarp door, my heart leapt. I gazed briefly at the young woman's feet, then at her midsection that was donned in an oversized new pair of underwear. Even though there was no need to look any further to confirm my worst fear, I looked at her face. The cartoonish prosthetic eyes that had replaced the victim's peered back at me as if mocking me.

"Mitchell, this is fucked up. This is going to be a fucking mess with the media. This case just took a left turn that we knew was coming, and I know for a fact that it won't stop until we do something about it. We have not one, not two, but three fucking bodies, and not a fucking clue as of yet. I can assure that she won't have a print on her." I was frustrated beyond belief.

We knew early on that we were dealing with serial killers based on the nature and details of the murders, but whoever was doing this was good, and that's what bothered me.

"Lane…Lane…Calm the heck down! We have to focus, and now is not the time to let this get you upset. Unfortunately, we knew this was coming," Mitchell stated as he grabbed my arm and pulled me aside. "Look, no one wants to ever deal with a case like this, but shit happens. You're the best A.P.D has in homicide for a reason. As of now, we don't have shit, but there is always evidence. We just have to find it, those are the words you always say to me."

I reached into my pocket and pulled out my cell phone. I called my supervisor, who was aware of the homicide, but unaware that this was similar to the investigation we were already a part of. Lt. Johnson blew his top, as expected, but said he would provide us with all necessary resources. I noticed our media relations representative heading in my direction. It was his job to provide as little information as possible, while providing enough information to cease questions. He had one of the most difficult jobs in the department, as he also covered shootings by officers.

"Is there anything specific you want us to put out there, Detective?" He always gave an officer a chance to start the narrative.

"Nothing specific, just give a basic statement right now. Deceased Caucasian female, discovered in the early morning, no identification as of yet…so on and so on," I told him.

"You got it," he answered back, before walking off to where the media rushed him like piranhas.

I couldn't hear what he was saying, so I moved closer. "Where are you going, Lane?" Mitchell called out to me

"I want to hear what he says, but I also want to see what the media knows, based on their questions." I let him know.

I walked up just in time to catch his opening remarks. "At 5:35 a.m., the Atlanta Police Department responded to a call sending them to the corner of Apple Street and Leonard, about a person reported as unresponsive. It was discovered that an unidentified female was located and declared deceased on the scene. The cause of death is pending an autopsy from the medical examiner's office. The identity and other specifics of this case are still developing and unavailable right now. The Atlanta Police Homicide Unit will be continuing the investigation from this point," he added.

"So, this is a homicide investigation," one reporter stated. I watched him maneuver around with ease.

"Anytime we find a person deceased, homicide will always take a look."

"How was she killed?" another reporter shot out.

"We're very early in our investigation, that question is undetermined at this time. That's all for now. We'll update as we can, thank you for your time," he concluded before walking away.

I noticed a woman standing in the distance, quietly taking in the scene and eating an ice cream. Who enjoys a death scene with an ice cream? I asked myself It didn't sit right with me.

"Hey, Mitchell, come here for a second. Look at me and me only while I speak to you."

"What's going on, Lane?"

"At your eleven o'clock, there is a woman wearing shades and eating an ice cream. She looks out of place for some reason. Where would she get an ice cream this early in the morning is my first question, and why would she be enjoying it at a crime scene is my second question. I want you to cover me as I approach her without drawing attention to us as I do."

"I got you covered." He turned and followed me with his eyes as I headed in the woman's direction. Upon seeing me, she licked her ice cream then turned to walk away. She maneuvered to the crowd slowly. "Hey, can I help you with something?" I asked her, but she didn't acknowledge me at all. That eerie feeling continued to creep up inside of me, and I started to walk faster toward this unexpected guest, and Mitchell quickly caught on.

Our fast paced walk turned into a trot and before we knew it, after turning a corner, the woman was gone. I placed my hand on my weapon and tried to figure out where she could have gone. There was no car for her to jump into and make a get away, and there was no door for her to run into as this was a residential area.

I radioed Mitchell. "Hey, get some cruisers to cover a couple of blocks to see if they see the woman I was telling you about," I told him.

"Can you give me a better description of her, Lane? I barely saw her. What did you see that makes you want to pursue her? We need to get back over to the crime scene."

Mitchell was right. I placed my radio back on my belt, and did one last glance around the area, but I was sure whoever the woman was, was long gone by now.

I made it back to the crime scene and the Chief M.E. Leggett was on the scene. "Good morning," she greeted me with a huge hug.

"It's good to see you girl, even if it is here. How have things been? We haven't spoken since you called on the day we visited your office." I was happy to see her, but looking at her, I could tell that she was going through something, and it wasn't something minor either.

"There's been so much going on, but please, let's catch up later; the last thing I need is a breakdown at work." She confirmed my suspicion.

"I understand. Have you looked at the body yet?" I changed the subject.

"I have, and everything so far is the same. I've had them process the body, and I informed them to get it back to the office. I know that these bodies are starting to pile up, and I can promise you that I will find something…I always do."

"I believe you. Mitchell and I are going to head back to the office. I will give you a call this evening for us to talk, and we'll be by the office tomorrow." I left her to do her job, then went over to Mitchell.

"What did the Chief M.E. say?"

"She said that it's the same, which we already knew, and that she'll see us tomorrow. I can't get that lady out of my mind, Mitchell, she fits Special Agent Mae's description to the letter."

"If that's the case, we need to get back to the precinct and have a sketch artist put to paper what you saw. Maybe we will get a hit in CODIS."

Mitchell and I left the crime scene to the technicians and the Chief M.E. to gather all the evidence. Back at the precinct, we were met by Special Agent Mae, as news had made it to her about the recent turn of events.

"Would you like me to get you a better chair?" Mitchell asked her. She was sitting next to my desk in a plastic and metal chair.

"I'm fine. I just came by to talk to you guys for a minute off the record." With the recent turn of events, I felt a little intimidated but thankful that she had shown up.

"I, for one, am thankful that you dropped by, as I believe I caught a glimpse of one of our suspects." Mitchell looked at me incredulously.

"Don't, Lane," he tried to stop me.

"Lane, what are you talking about? What did you see today?"

"This morning while we processed the scene, I decided to see how our media specialist handled distributing information to the media, but also to see what the media themselves knew. While doing so, I happened to see a woman standing in the crowd eating an ice cream cone. It struck me to be odd, as it was a little after 8 a.m. She fit the profile that you gave us, so I decided to investigate. As I approached her, she began to walk away, moving through the crowd with ease. From that point, I still had eyes on her, but then she took off in a trot and turned the corner. From there, I lost her."

"Interesting," she simply replied. Not the response that I was looking for.

"Well, what do you think, Special Agent Mae?" Mitchell questioned, shaking his head with doubt in his tone.

"So, Mitchell, you don't think that it's a possibility that our killers could have been at the scene today, and Lane actually got a glimpse of one of them?" Special Agent Mae wanted to confirm.

"I'm not saying that she didn't see anyone that was out of place, but when I think of the magnitude of this crime, the care in which these women are laid out, I find it highly unlikely that our suspects would stick around. That would mean the vehicle that our victim was disposed of would've been close by. We did a canvas of the area looking for large vehicles like our first witness described hearing." His points were all valid, but not open minded, and from what I knew of Special Agent Mae, she was about to enlighten him.

"Mitchell, I do thank you for your candid assertions. I must say under normal circumstances I would agree with you, but these aren't normal circumstances; we are looking for serial killers. Do you know that most serial killers have the IQ of a genius?

"There is nothing, and I mean nothing, that they think they can't get away with. When I hear about the possibility of one or both of the suspects being there, I can believe it. Killers get a thrill out of watching their 'work,' as most claim. In this case, we are literally having circles run around us, so it's very plausible that their confidence is high enough to show up."

"That's not confidence to me, that's insanity," Mitchell countered

"Call it what you want, but let me ask you this. Have you ever snuck out of the house as a kid through the window or backdoor?"

Mitchell looked at me as if I were going to answer for him. "Of course, who hasn't?" he replied

"And when doing so, you had a routine or a time that you knew you wouldn't get caught, right?" Mitchell nodded. I knew where she was going with this. "That routine never changed until you got caught, which was probably by accident like when you were sneaking back in." Mitchell let out a laugh.

"You see, this is the same thing. At the moment, they have no reason to change anything that they're doing because the threat of being caught hasn't been there. I can assure you, that will change soon." I was looking at Special Agent Lizzie Mae with so much respect and admiration. The way she broke that down simply convinced Mitchell to nod his head in agreement.

"I feel much better after hearing your words of affirmation. I now have an image in my head to go off. I'm about to go to our sketch artist and have him draw her up, so we can get some eyes on her if possible." I stood up to leave, but Special Agent Mae grabbed my hand.

"Do you hear yourself? Slow down young lady. Do you think

putting out a sketch at this point is wise? I mean, let's be realistic. Do you actually think that the woman you saw wasn't in a disguise or wig? You now have something that no one has, and that is a potential description on how this person walks, runs, and what her lips look as you watched her eat an ice cream."

Once again she was right. I hadn't thought about it in that way. "I can't thank you enough for being a mentor and to go with this case. I can see why you are one of the best at what you do." I gave her praise.

"Likewise Detective Lane. You are making a name for yourself with your handling of this case. You and Mitchell will make heads of this thing, and like I told you before, trust your policing skills and instincts."

CHAPTER TWENTY-SIX

MISTER

After my conversation with Missy, I didn't feel that we could just sit back and let Detective Lane gain ground on who we were. I accessed the file that Missy had stored in the computer, then took one of her vehicles and left. I knew that she would want to kill me if she knew what I was doing, but it was all for her. If they knew who she was, that would mean that I could lose her, and that was a risk I just couldn't take. I grabbed the information that I needed then decided to head out.

I watched the young black girl hanging out at the popular outdoor market place, with a small crowd of her friends, enjoying life without a care in the world. They lingered around their motor scooters laughing, and taking photos. From where I stood, it would have been easy to send a headshot to each one of them before the other dropped, and no one would be the wiser. This was about the detective and so this had to be a statement so that she would have no reason to doubt the message. I assembled my drone and came out from the shadows.

I followed the group of women from a good distance as I flew my drone in front of me. I watched them park the scooters, then continue straight to where the parking garage was. They stopped briefly before taking the elevator and asked someone to take a picture of them. The elevator door opened, and they proceeded inside.

I tossed the remote to the drone, and the drone followed in a crash behind me as I ran to the stairs. At each floor, I opened the door slightly to see if I would see them. Finally, on the fourth floor, I saw them giving each other hugs and saying their goodbyes.

I kept my head down as I was well aware of the cameras placed throughout. I blended in with others taking photos and filming the historic area. The detective's daughter pulled her keys out of her purse, and placed them in her left hand. She kept her hand in her purse, which let me know that she was possibly armed or carrying something for self defense. I walked in the opposite direction of her allowing her to make it to her car without fail. She engaged the alarm, then looked back at me, as I continued to walk. She would have to drive past the lift gate, and when she let her window down, I would strike.

I backed up between an SUV sitting in a handicap zone and another vehicle and waited patiently. I noticed a car pulling into the entrance, and I could easily make out that it was an unmarked police car. The driver was a male, but when I locked my eyes on the passenger, I dropped down to my knees. I put my knife up and pulled out my gun.

I couldn't believe my eyes. This had to be my lucky day as I watched Detective Lane, and who I knew had to be her partner, drive around to where her daughter was parked and blocked her in. My mind was racing telling me to get out of there.

The daughter got out of her car, and I could see her throw her hands up in frustration. Detective Lane got out of the passenger side and was explaining something that ended up calming the young girl. They moved close as if they were about to embrace. If I was going to make a move, now was the time.

I took a position to where I had both of them in my sight. I aimed for the back of the young girl. I took a few deep breaths, then I let off two rounds.

"What the fuck!" The driver had opened his door causing them to look at him and my shots went whisking past them. I watched them drop to the ground, and the male looked in my direction and returned fire.

I ran with my head low out into the evening where people were walking up and down the street. Anyone in my way got knocked to the ground. I could hear the engine of the police car as it bussed through the liftgate in pursuit. Sirens came from a distance, and I realized that I hadn't planned for all of this.

I turned the corner and saw a group of teens mulling around, just as the car came to a screech at the corner. I grabbed one of the young girls by her hair, then placed her in front of me as a shield as I tried my best to remain behind her.

"Let the girl go!" I heard the detective yell out from behind the car door; her weapon pointed in my direction. "This is not going to end well for you, so let her go!"

"It's going to end how I want it to end!" I knew I didn't have much time left before I was surrounded and in a no win situation, so I did what my military instincts called for and that was to initiate the attack.

I squeezed the young girl by the back of her neck and lifted her off the ground then slung her down in front of me and let off three shots, before taking off running. Shots were being fired in my direction, and then a burning began in my shoulder. I pushed, leapt over, and ran through anything in my way until I knew no one was behind me. I was breathing hard and knew I had to calm myself down and think. I found a place to stop behind a liquor store on Ponce De Leon street, then did my best to stop the bleeding. I had taken a round to my shoulder that went straight through. I ripped a piece of my shirt, stuffed the small hole, then wrapped it. That would have to do for now.

I pulled out my phone and called Missy. She was livid, but concerned with my well-being. She instructed me as to where to meet her.

"What in fuck were you thinking?" She lit into me as soon as I got in the backseat of the vehicle and laid down. "Are you fucking crazy or something? I told you not to do anything!"

"I had no choice, they were coming after us regardless of what you say." The pain was starting to set in.

"Well they now have your DNA, and you didn't kill anyone, which sucks."

"I'm not finished either."

"You're so fucking hard headed. We will deal with Detective Lane, that's for sure. When you go looking for trouble, you find it."

I felt relieved as Missy was now on board to do what needed to be done. I knew that my DNA would show up once it ran through the veteran database. At this point, it didn't matter, there was nothing that we couldn't afford to get that I needed, even surgery.

CHAPTER TWENTY-SEVEN
DETECTIVE LANE

"Mitchell, make a call out for several medics, we need to get this woman checked out for injuries as well. I have a suspicion he was one of our killers, or he knows who they are." I was thankful that the monster didn't shoot the young woman. He did manage to literally scare the shit out of her.

"This is fucking crazy, Lane. Are you okay?" Mitchell asked me, trying to catch his breath.

"Yeah, I'm fine. Damn, we were so close. Where is June?" I asked him, looking around to see if I saw her. Cops were everywhere now, as well as medics attending to the people that the large man had injured.

I had to pull myself together immediately. I started processing mental notes on what I saw and was replaying the scene in my head. My thoughts were interrupted by June running up behind me, and throwing her arms around my neck. She was in tears.

"Mom…what is going on?" I could feel her shaking, and I was thankful for my motherly instincts that made me check her location. When I saw that she was close, I asked Mitchell to go to her.

"I believe that was one of the people that we are looking for, and if it was, that means that they know who you are," I told her. "I know you were mad about me showing up here tonight unexpectedly, but another body was discovered, and my concern for you or your friends is at an all time high."

June wiped the tears from her eyes. I could see the strength in her returning. "Mom, they need to be off the streets, and if anybody can make that happen, it's you."

"I will, baby. I need you to stay with one of your friends tonight. I will have an officer follow you, and have officers on rotation until we figure something out. Don't worry, this will not be our life," I assured her. " I need to go."

"I know, Mom, just be safe please." I headed over to Mitchell.

"How is she?" I saw his concern as he watched her being escorted back to her car.

"She was shaken up, as expected, but she was fine by the time we finished talking. It's obvious now that they think we know something we don't know."

"I believe I hit him, Lane. We need to secure a sample to be processed."

"He was fast Mitchell, I have never seen that before. There are only a couple people that could move with that kind of speed and agility and the height and weight that he possessed."

"Athletes and soldiers." He was on point with my assertion.

"I have a feeling that he was the latter. Did you see his face when he held the girl hostage? His face was disfigured, it looked like it might have been burned or damaged in an accident."

"We need to get back to the office. I'll inform the officers that samples of the blood found need to be processed into the lab with your name on it."

"Thank you. I'll provide a statement to the investigating officer, so we can get out of here when you get back."

I gave my statement, and Mitchell and I headed back to the precinct where Special Agent Mae said she would meet us. I was silent the entire ride as I kept thinking about how June's life could have been taken had we not shown up. It was more than personal at this point, as they had made an attempt on my daughter's life.

"Yes...yes...I told you guys that pressure will make the most detail-oriented person make a mistake." She greeted us as we made it to my desk at the same time. "I had a feeling that you were right when you said that you saw one of the suspects. That, in turn, caused them to want to know who is investigating them, which is common amongst serial killers. There have been instances where the killings have stopped in certain cities due to who the investigator ends up being."

As Special Agent Mae spoke, my mind drifted. Usually, I would be latching on to every word that came out of her mouth, but not today.

"Lane, Mitchell…in my office now!" Lt. Johnson's voice boomed as he gave us an order.

"Do you need me to come with you guys?" Special Agent Mae offered.

"Might as well, that way we don't have to repeat everything over again once we come out," Mitchell answered for me.

We filed into Lt. Johnson's office like kids going into the principal's office. Although we had done nothing wrong, I sure felt like it since the suspect got away.

"Can you explain to me how our suspects managed to keep getting out of these grids that we have set up to prevent them from escaping? This is your show, and I've given you all the resources you need."

Why did he start with me? If I knew, they would be in custody. I wasn't in the mood for the Lieutenant's bullshit today, and I was about to let him have it.

"Sir, may I interject?" Special agent Mae requested. Divine intervention I reasoned.

"Sure, these two act as if they can't talk." He was upset for no reason in my eyes.

"A couple of weeks ago, Detective Lane spotted someone that fit the profile that we have on file, which you already know about. I'm sure that you are familiar with criminals trying to scare someone off a case. In this case, Lane happened to see something that she wasn't supposed to see, which we don't know."

"What do you think that is, Lane, because I have a meeting with the superintendent. I need to have something that makes some fucking sense, other than the serial killers are now following our detectives. Do you know how foolish we would look if word got out that while we're out looking for them, they are trailing us?"

He had a point. "Like Special Agent Mae stated, I saw something that day, and that woman knows it. I keep replaying the entire scene in my head…her walk, her look, her lips, her hair, it had to be something, but what… I don't know. Right now my focus is on the disfigured giant that nearly took a woman out, and moved with the speed and agility unlike I've ever witnessed before."

"Do you think you can describe him to our sketch artist?" the Lieutenant questioned.

"I can, his face is unforgettable," I replied, while Mitchell elaborated.

"This guy wasn't average to say the least, Lieutenant. I watched him lift the young girl off the ground with one hand and toss her to the ground. He fired a couple of shots in our direction, and I returned fire. The guy took off into a full sprint out into where the public was, knocking over everything in sight. He leapt over the hood of a car as if it was a small fence. Have you ever seen or heard of anything like this?" Mitchell posed the question to Special Agent Mae.

"Can't say I have. The description that you're giving me, makes me think that this guy might be a military experiment gone wrong." No one found it funny. "All jokes aside, I think we are dealing with a former soldier, and one that was well trained; a marine or special forces possibly. With that being said, I think you need to look at veterans with service connected disabilities."

"I believe him to be military as well. We are also having his blood run through the lab as we speak. It won't be long before we know exactly who this creep is," I informed them.

"Everything is starting to make sense now, Lane. The woman does her part with ruse, and the man is the enforcer, or the one who subdues the victims. With his appearance, he is most likely sitting somewhere close until he is notified to intervene," Special Agent Mae explained.

"I hear everything that you said, Lane, and I think it would be wise to get you and your daughter to a safe location. I'll put Jones and Moreno on the case until we can get a bead of these clowns. Lane, you and Mitchell need to get over to the sketch artist so that we can get out a composite of our suspects. As of now, you can focus on you and your daughter."

It sounded like he was taking me off the case or sending me into hiding. "With all due respect Lieutenant, these people came after me. If you take me off the case, they'll do the same to the next detective. Yes, I do want protection for my daughter and I, but removing me from this case would be a huge mistake," I advised.

"I agree with her, Lieutenant. You and I have been doing this long enough to know when you're about to hit paydirt with a case. It always gets worse before it gets better. I can assure you that Detective Lane and Mitchell are your best hope in getting these people off the streets. You can't take her or Mitchell off the case, and if you do, I can assure you that I will make sure to let my superiors know I disagreed."

I truly appreciated Special Agent Mae's words of affirmation and support. She had a way of making me believe in myself. Being in a male dominated field isn't easy, but it's women like Special Agent Mae who do their best to make sure we are heard and not dismissed.

"Fine, you're staying on the case, but no gungho stuff. Do you hear me?"

I heard him loud and clear, but did he hear me when I said that he went after my daughter? If he did, then he'd know there was nothing he could say that would stop me from enacting justice.

ACKNOWLEDGMENTS

Foremost, I would like to thank my Lord and Savior, Jesus, for giving me the strength to write this novel.

As I created this novel, 'Never Cry Alone', hard times were upon PlaTy Multimedia and Publishing. I can't thank my team consisting of Alan Little, James Scales, and Elizabeth M. Johnson, along with mentor and fellow author, CJ Lopez, for holding things down when it got tough for us as a company. PlaTy Multimedia and Publishing grew, and flourished in those times, and for that I'm forever grateful. We lost loved ones, had personal tragedies, and took losses. So, with all sincerity, I would truly like to thank each and every one of you guys for your support while I was in that transitional phase.

As a team, PlaTy Multimedia is back and more focused than ever, and we're ready to continue with the mission of promoting literacy. That mission comes with tons of support, and as much as I would like to acknowledge everyone, I realistically can't. I do appreciate the private talks, the outings, the words of affirmation, the trips, and the genuine love from the circle I have now.

I would like to give a special thanks to my mom Valencia, my Pops Anthony, my sis Taress J. --the real G.O.A.T, my bro Tyrone Plair, my son Darren, my Aunt Tracy Lewis, and my grandkids. This has been a long process, but we've maintained it as a family and will continue to do so. Thank you all!!!

To my church family, thank you for all of your prayers and support, I love you all.

I would like to add a special thanks to my co-author and business partner, Elizabeth M. Johnson. Thank you for your hard work as Chief Operating Officer for PlaTy Multimedia and Publishing. Your hard work and dedication have never wavered.

ABOUT THE AUTHOR

Born in the Windy City of Chicago, Tyrell Plair knew that the wind would blow his way one day, even if he had to create the breeze. But that breeze would eventually lead him and his family to Pensacola, Florida, where Tyrell gained a love for reading and writing. In middle school, he began writing rap lyrics to recite, and poetry for fun, but then he began to love it. He then started writing poetry for his male classmates, and the rest is history.

Throughout the years, Tyrell has honed those skills that he developed at an early age as a writer by ghostwriting novels, penning screenplays, and adding film directing to his resume. In 2019, he released his debut novel, "Stolen Innocence," as an independent author. After enduring the struggles that most self-published authors go through, Tyrell decided to look at writing and producing novels as a business. With this newfound information and passion inside, it was only right that he used his knowledge and platform to grow as a writer and help others as well. Tyrell formed what he would name PlaTy Multimedia and Publishing, and would release his first novel coauthored with Elizabeth M. Johnson titled "Just Like My Dad."

Tyrell earned his Bachelor of Science in Applied Psychology with a Concentration in Media and Technology from the University of Phoenix. He has written and produced commercials for The Outrageous Love Foundation, L & J Multicultural Barbershop in Pensacola Florida, and other film projects.

He has released several novels from other authors under his PlaTy Multimedia and Publishing Imprint that includes Mamaw Mel's Kitchen, A Christmas Battle, Beguiled, and Beneath the Surface of the Skin.

Tyrell is a person set on ensuring literacy is promoted everywhere it can be. When not writing or leading PlaTy Multimedia and Publishing, you can find him playing a game of chess, working out, fishing, or reading.

Stolen Innocence

www.ingramcontent.com/pod-product-compliance
Lightning Source LLC
Chambersburg PA
CBHW061307210726

48293CB00003B/1146